LEAVING EDGEFIELD

LEAVING EDGEFIELD

CARRIE BUTLER'S STORY

a novel

CAROLYN W. HOOKER

EVENING POST
BOOKS

Published by
Evening Post Books
Charleston, South Carolina
www.eveningpostbooks.com

Author: Carolyn Hooker
Cover and Layout design: Danna Mathias Steele

Front Cover: The Miriam and Ira D. Wallach Division of Art, Prints and
Photographs: Photography Collection, The New York Public Library. "Negro
sharecropper's farmstead against the levee. Near Lake Providence, Louisiana"
New York Public Library Digital Collections.

First printing 2024.
Printed in the United States of America.

A CIP catalog record for this book has been applied
for from the Library of Congress.

ISBN: 979-8-9909493-6-2 (Paperback)

Evening Post Books is the Book division of Evening Post Publishing — proud publishers of the Pulitzer Prize winning *Post and Courier*, along with more than ten other independent newspapers across South Carolina.

When you purchase an Evening Post Book, you're supporting a community of local, independent editors, designers, authors, booksellers, and the nonprofits that several of our titles support.

Thank you for investing in the power of the written word, the value of traditional publishing, and the people who bring it to life.

Learn more about EPB and follow the journey:

🌐 eveningpostbooks.com
📷 @eveningpostbooks

PRAISE FOR *LEAVING EDGEFIELD*

"*Leaving Edgefield* is an absolutely beautiful novel, full of unquestionably genuine souls fighting to maintain dignity, faith, and affection in their lives. You will feel their love, fall into their hope, ache from their pain, and experience the fullness of their humanity in this remarkable story about one family's fight to stay together and control their destiny."

— JEFFERY BLOUNT, AUTHOR OF *MR. JIMMY FROM AROUND THE WAY* AND WINNER OF THE NEXT GENERATION INDIE BOOK AWARDS FOR AFRICAN AMERICAN FICTION

"There is scant information to be found about Essie Mae Washington Williams's mother, Carrie Butler, who was a teenager working as a maid in the Thurmond household when she became pregnant. *Leaving Edgefield* gives voice to Carrie Butler. Carolyn Hooker has written an important story, one that extends to the deepest roots of inequity in the American South and brings to the surface the unacknowledged trauma countless women domestic workers have endured while trying to earn a living in the well-appointed homes of the South's most powerful families."

— MICHELE MOORE, AUTHOR OF *THE CIGAR FACTORY* AND FINALIST FOR THE BELLWETHER PRIZE FOR LITERATURE

"Carolyn Hooker writes with courage, imagination, and keen insight, and the result is a haunting tale of unflinching motherly love despite often crippling powerlessness. From the first page of *Leaving Edgefield*, there's an urgency in Carrie Butler's story that will stay with readers long after the last, perfectly nuanced sentence. Hooker is a masterful, empathetic story teller and *Leaving Edgefield* is a triumph you'll not soon forget."

— Michel Stone, MEd, Author of
The Iguana Tree and *Border Child*

"*Leaving Edgefield* beautifully and authentically depicts the story of Carrie Butler, the mother of Strom Thurmond's bi-racial daughter, Essie Mae Washington-Williams. Until this well-researched work of historical fiction, no one has imagined the story of Carrie, a helpless teenager in the 1920s who matures into a courageous woman able to save herself and her daughter. Carrie and the people who help shape her life come alive with the depth of human emotion in this extraordinary story."

— Susan Beckham Zurenda, author of *The Girl From the Red Rose Motel*

For Marie, Jesse, Frankie, and Mark

TABLE OF CONTENTS

AUTHOR'S NOTE

Leaving Edgefield is a historical fiction novel based on the life of Carrie Butler (1910-1948), the mother of J. Strom Thurmond's bi-racial daughter, Essie Mae Washington-Williams. While information abounds on almost every aspect of Thurmond's life, reliable information about Carrie Butler is scarce. So, to piece together events of Butler's life, I've located census records housed at the Edgefield County Historical Society; birth and death records of Butler, her parents, and her siblings on Ancestry.com; bits and pieces about Butler on the Internet; information in her daughter's memoir, *Dear Senator: A Memoir by the Daughter of Strom Thurmond;* as well as references to Butler in numerous books and articles about Thurmond himself. Based on findings from these sources, *Leaving Edgefield* weaves together real-life events with educated and intentional imagination to picture the interaction that occurred between her and Thurmond.

To date, no one has told Carrie Butler's story, one that deserves to be told, one not entirely unlike that of Sally Hemings. Although after Senator Thurmond died in 2003 at the age of 100, and the daughter, Essie Mae Washington-Williams, publicly revealed Thurmond to be her father, her mother, Butler, has remained virtually unknown. As evidence of her obscurity, when a friend of mine was visiting the Edgefield County Historical Society recently and she told a local visitor there about my book, he remarked,

"Why would anyone write a book about her? She was nobody." Carrie Butler *was* somebody. Culturally relegated to a position of social, gender, racial, economic, and age inferiority, and ravaged by the disease that took her life at age thirty-eight, she nevertheless left a legacy through her daughter whose life was one of distinction. I hope *Leaving Edgefield* is a fitting tribute that memorializes Carrie Butler's life.

Prologue

CARRIE BUTLER EMERGED FROM A CAB INTO RAIN NEAR THE curb at the General Hospital of Philadelphia, November 1948. She looked down to watch her step and noticed there in the gutter a piece of broken glass, a milky lime green, washed clean by water rushing toward a storm drain, and the word *celadon* surfaced from her memory. She had learned that word years earlier in her schoolroom in the Tabernacle Church basement in Augusta, Georgia, when one afternoon during recess in the churchyard, Carrie pulled her teacher over to show her a bright green moth of that same color, as big as her teacher's hand, its delicate wings opened, motionless and flat against the bark of a tree. The other children huddled around Miss Velma who leaned in to examine the insect, telling her pupils, "It's a Luna moth. It just emerged from its cocoon and it's drying its wings," then asking them, "What do you see that makes it different from other moths?"

"It's green!"

"It has a long tail!"

"It has fuzzy antennas!"

Back inside, Miss Velma told the children they were lucky to have seen a Luna moth. "They fly mostly at night and have a brief lifespan – little more than a week!" She described its color as "celadon" and went on to tell them about that transparent green glaze that originated in China, about Luna being the name of the Roman moon goddess, about the plural of *antenna* being *antennae*, all things connected to other wondrous things in the little school-room beneath the floorboards of the sanctuary back in 1920.

Carrie moved toward the hospital entrance as fast as she was able to, considering the pain in her back and sides. Someone at the door helped her with her coat and got her a towel to dry her face and arms and the receptionist began checking her in.

"May I have your name and birth date, Miss?"

"Carrie Butler Clark. September 18, 1910."

"And why are you here today, Mrs. Clark?"

"I passed out at work. I have kidney disease."

A few more questions, then the receptionist told her, "Please have a seat and someone will come for you." After Carrie found an empty chair, she became aware of the other people sitting in the narrow room — one, a pregnant girl staring at the wall in front of her. Eventually, a nurse wearing a white pinafore and a cap pinned to the back of her head rolled a wheelchair over to Carrie. She helped Carrie into the chair, then turned and guided her down the hall. They entered a small alcove, where the nurse pulled a curtain closed behind them.

"Dr. Drexler will be here soon. Let's get you out of these wet clothes and onto the table. Cover you up, get you warm. We'll keep your clothes and pocketbook under your bed until you're ready to go home."

Carrie felt nauseated. She raised her arms for the nurse to wrest her damp dress and her slip up over her head. For Carrie, "going home" now meant seeing her mother again, her father, and her dear sister Mae, all of whom had died years ago back in Edgefield.

Carrie had just closed her eyes when Dr. Drexler pushed the curtain back and greeted her. The nurse helped her sit up while he paused to read the few notes the receptionist had made in Carrie's chart. He took her swollen hands in his and turned them over to look at her palms, noting the gold wire band pressing into the flesh of her ring finger, her swollen feet, her bloated abdomen.

"I'll order tests for you tomorrow, Mrs. Clark. Nurse Fisher will bring you something for pain." He held her left arm, turned it over, and tapped the inside of her elbow as the nurse suspended a glass bottle from a metal pole. Carrie watched a clear liquid drip from the bottle into rubber tubing that snaked down to the needle he had slipped into her vein. The doctor signed papers to admit her, stood, touched her shoulder, then moved on.

The nurse helped Carrie back into the wheelchair, grasped the metal pole with one hand, gathered up the rubber tubing, then proceeded to wheel Carrie to the poverty ward. Younger nurses nodded respectfully at Nurse Fisher as they passed through a corridor and into the long room where narrow beds lined both walls, maybe four feet separating one from the next. Odors of sick people mixed with fumes of traffic coming through open windows, and suddenly Carrie vomited. Nurse Fisher held a metal pan under her face, supported Carrie's forehead, as watery bile dripped from her mouth and nose. After a brief moment to rest, they continued past other patients — some asking for water, others requesting pain medicine — until they reached Carrie's bed near the open window.

It was urgent now that Carrie see Mrs. Sadie Alexander, a Philadelphia attorney for whom Carrie had altered business suits and dresses and, most recently, a silk evening gown that Mrs. Alexander had found in New York. A member of an illustrious family of Black doctors, lawyers, and educators, Mrs. Alexander had stood still while Carrie measured, marked, and pinned, and had drawn Carrie into conversations about her childhood and about her family. She had listened as Carrie talked about her daughter, Essie Mae, age sixteen, with whom she had only recently reunited, and about her son, Willie Clark, Junior, age ten.

"What about Willie Clark, Sr.?" Mrs. Alexander had asked Carrie.

"My husband stayed in Edgefield, South Carolina. It was complicated. Things down there he couldn't leave. When I moved up here, I started back using my maiden name, Butler. My legal name is Clark."

"Well, if you ever need any *legal* help, you let me know. My husband and I practice estate and family law. I'll be glad to help you."

Carrie needed her help now.

When Carrie fainted at work that afternoon as she was pinning a hem into place, Lola Taggart, her employer and owner of the alterations shop, excused herself from her own client, helped Carrie up and outside, hailed a cab, and paid the driver to take Carrie to Philadelphia General Hospital. Mrs. Taggart arrived that evening to see about Carrie. She brought her warm bread wrapped in a tea towel. Carrie held it on her stomach on top of the sheet. The warmth felt good in her hands.

"Thank you, Mrs. Taggart. Will you please let Mrs. Alexander know I'm in the hospital? Will you ask her if she will come see me?"

"Sure, I will, Carrie. She's coming for a fitting tomorrow. I'll tell her then. And I'll be back soon."

"Thank you."

The following evening, the head nurse in the poverty unit noticed a middle-aged woman moving toward her wearing a tailored suit and expensive-looking shoes and wondered if she was in the wrong ward. "May I help you?"

"Yes, I'm here to see Mrs. Carrie Butler, please. "

She looked at her patient list. "We don't have anybody by that name in this ward. You must be in the wrong area."

"Are you sure? I was told this afternoon that she's a patient here.

"We do have a Carrie Clark."

"Yes, that is she. I'd like to see Mrs. Clark, if I may."

"She's back this way," she said, leading Mrs. Alexander to Carrie. "We open these windows to let fresh air in here, but the fumes and noise of traffic come in, too." Mrs. Alexander fought the smell of bedpans that needed to be emptied and sheets that had been soiled throughout the day. "Here we are. She might be asleep. Mrs. Clark, you got a visitor. You awake? It's somebody here to see you. Let's put this pillow back here. Raise you up a little. Don't get worn out talking. I'll be back with your medicine in a little while."

"Thank you. Carrie? Hello, dear. It's Sadie Alexander. Lola told me you were here. She said you asked for me? You feel like having a visitor, Carrie? I'm here if you feel like a little company. I'm sorry you're not well."

Carrie opened her eyes and focused. "Mrs. Alexander. Oh, thank you. Thank you for coming. I need your help. It's for my daughter. I need some things written down. You told me one time if I needed help to let you know. I've got some money I can pay you…"

"Shhh, Carrie, no. I remember. Just tell me what you need."

"I told him I know you. I need you to write down what all happened so he has to keep his word. Even after I'm gone. I believe he'll do what he said he would. He's known for keeping his word. But I've got to make sure."

"Who is 'he,' Carrie? Is this about your husband?"

"No. My daughter's father. Essie Mae. Essie Mae's father is Strom Thurmond. From Edgefield. Where I'm from. I mentioned your name to him one time. That's all it took. He knows who you are."

"Strom Thurmond? The *governor* Strom Thurmond is your daughter's *father*? Strom Thurmond from South Carolina is *Essie Mae's father*?"

"Yes. And he promised to pay for her college if I didn't tell anybody."

"Tell anybody?"

"That he's her daddy. And now he's running for President, maybe you could let him know you've talked to me. Tonight, here in Philadelphia, I know it's about over. I'm not afraid. Sometimes I'm afraid. I hope when it happens, I won't feel like I'm drowning. I have to make sure Essie Mae will get to finish college. He's been paying for it. He's got to keep on until she graduates. Will you help me see he does?"

"Of course, I'll help you. I'll need you to explain some things to me. I'll come straight from court tomorrow and you can tell me everything you want me to know. Go back as far as you want – it's all important."

"Thank you, Mrs. Alexander. I'll tell you everything tomorrow. You got to keep in touch with Essie Mae, see if he's still paying for her college. If he stops, you got to tell him you knew me. Tell him I was your personal seamstress. Tell him I told you everything."

Chapter One

Thank you for coming back, Mrs. Alexander. I'm gonna start with when my folks sent me to live with my aunt in Augusta, Georgia. That was in 1918. I was eight years old, and I stayed there until I was fourteen, just going back once when my daddy died. I didn't realize it at that time, but living those years with my aunt would turn out to be one of the best things that happened to me in my childhood.

The evening they told me they had to send me away, I begged them not to, but I had no say-so in the matter. Me and my sister Mary had been sitting on the front step watching for Mama and Daddy to get back from the field. Right about sundown, when we saw them coming, we ran down the road to meet them. Daddy had got Mama a soda at Reel's on the way home because her stomach was unsettled. Mama must've been just barely pregnant with my little brother Willis. He had wrapped a rag around the bottle to keep it cold and Mama had saved some for us. Me and Mary finished it off, then skipped ahead and back to them, barefooted on that dusty road, chasing the lightning bugs that had started blinking all around us. I caught one and scraped it from my finger into the empty soda bottle. Mary pinched the tail off one she'd caught, smeared that powdery gold stuff on her finger, and held her hand up in my face to show me her "diamond ring," telling me, "Look! I'm getting married." Once we reached our yard, Mama told Mary, "You go ahead and see about the young'uns inside and get their supper on the table" and told me, "Carrie, come sit here with us a minute, baby." Mama and Daddy sat down on either side of me on the front step. Mama took the rag she'd had around her soda bottle and wiped dirt off her face and throat. Daddy took ahold of my hand and said, "Baby, I know you don't remember your Aunt Lucy, but me and your mama need to send one of y'all to stay with her for a while. It won't be for good. We think you the one will get along there best of all."

I leaned my head forward like I hadn't heard him right and whispered, "Say *what?*" Mama started explaining, but all I heard was noise. When I realized what they were telling me, I pulled away. "I ain't going! I can't leave y'all! I don't even *know* her!" I slung Mama's hand off my arm and ran out into the yard and stood there, trying to catch my breath 'til Daddy came and stood behind me.

He told me, "It won't be for long. Things going to get better around here before you know it." Then he hugged me into him. He told me, "Tunch," – that's what they called me back then – "you know school here don't run but a few months a year, but in Augusta they run maybe six months out the year. You'll come back here so smart you can teach the rest of us how to read good and write real pretty and help me keep 'count of what I'm owed." My daddy never had been to school a day in his life, but couldn't nobody keep account of their money any better than he could.

Mama came and stood by Daddy. "Aunt Lucy's niece, Velma, lives with her, too, and she's a teacher. You'll go to her school. You won't be gone long. Just 'til things get better here." She took my shoulders and I leaned into her, pressing my face into her dress.

"I won't eat so much." I plead. "Mae and Mattie can have half my food." I'm hurting so bad. Daddy touched my back, and I kicked his leg. I kicked my *daddy*.

End of that summer is when I left. Daddy woke me up before daylight, seemed like we had just gone to sleep. Mama walked out to the wagon with us, and when Daddy went to help me up, he had to pull me apart from Mama. I know she stood there in the dark to watch us leave, but once I got up in the wagon, I wouldn't look back.

That long ride from Edgefield to Augusta took all day. Aunt Lucy lived in the Laney-Walker neighborhood on Burke Street just south of downtown Augusta. Once we got there, I wouldn't budge off the wagon seat. Daddy put his arm around me, and we sat still in the heat, not saying anything, 'til he got down and held up his arms for me to come on.

About then Aunt Lucy burst out the screen door. She rushed to meet us and hugged Daddy with one arm and me with the other, pulling us both into her. "Oh law, Jasper! This child is pretty! Like her mama! She'll be grown tall as me next time you see her. Come here, baby, and let me see you. I got supper almost ready for y'all in the kitchen." Aunt Lucy led us inside her big house where it was cool and dark. I took Daddy's hand and followed behind her.

Aunt Lucy told Daddy, "I'm making a special dinner for Carrie's first night. Surely, you gonna stay here tonight, see she gets settled in before you have to go back in the morning." I looked to see how he would answer, and I was thrilled when he said he would stay. I thought about Mama, though, knew she would be worried 'til Daddy got back home.

At dinner, Aunt Lucy brought out bowls of food to the table, and the boarders who stayed at Lucy's house gathered round. I sat between Daddy and Lucy's niece, Velma. I watched how Velma put her napkin and her left hand in her lap and did the same. Everybody had plenty to eat, something we hadn't experienced at home in a long time. I helped Velma and Aunt Lucy clear off the table and wash and dry all the dishes, Aunt Lucy talking the whole time, telling me how she and my daddy played together when they were little. Velma got Daddy a blanket for him to sleep on a cot out on the porch. Aunt Lucy took me upstairs to where she had set me up a bed in the hall, just outside her own bedroom, and moved a small cabinet up next to it for me to keep my things in. That night when Lucy started to snore, I tiptoed downstairs and out onto the porch, climbed in the cot by Daddy and slept the rest of the night next to him.

———•———

You know, Carrie, I stayed with my Uncle Lewis to go to high school in Washington, DC. Even though I was about fourteen, I was reluctant to leave home, too.

Were your folks having a hard time feeding everyone at home?

No, Carrie, and I'm sorry your family struggled for food. How did you feel the next morning? Things often seem better once morning comes.

Yes, I felt steadier once it was daylight and I smelled the breakfast Aunt Lucy had cooked, two good meals in a row now. We sat down to eat and Daddy answered Aunt Lucy's questions about Mama and the rest of the children. I didn't cry when I watched him climb up in the wagon to go back home without me until I saw him take out his handkerchief and press his own eyes.

Chapter Two

Some nights here are more peaceful than others, Mrs. Alexander, but once daylight comes in through that window over there, I'm relieved that the night is over. Patients start talking quietly to the nurse, accepting the pills and water she's giving them, most voices low, just a humming sound. But most mornings I can hear a girl a few beds down from mine asking for her daddy. She looks about fifteen. I think about my own daddy. My father was Jasper Butler. He was born in 1855, twenty years older than Mama, on Edgewood Plantation and belonged to United States Senator Andrew Pickens Butler. After the war he was a share-cropper. He grew cotton, corn, sorghum — sometimes melons — on land belonged to a Mr. Arthur Robinson. Mr. Arthur got two thirds of what Daddy grew, sold the other third. From the money he got from that, he took out for the cost of tools and seed Daddy had put on credit at Reel's, then paid Daddy whatever was left. Sometimes it wasn't much of anything left.

One year Daddy had a good yield, better than he'd had the past few years. He always kept account of what he owed at Mr. Reel's and had figured he was going to come out good this time. It was probably late October one morning when I woke up with Mary poking me in the back, whispering, "Daddy said we can go with him to settle up with Mr. Arthur, then we going to Reel's, and he's go' let us buy something." I got right up, quiet not to wake up the others. Mama was sitting in the kitchen with her elbows on the table and her hands wrapped around her coffee cup. She was looking at Daddy as she sipped her coffee, her eyes smiling a little, unusual for her. Going out the door, Daddy told Mama she looked pretty sitting there, making her smile again.

As he hitched up the wagon, Mary climbed in, grabbed my hand and pulled me up. Daddy got in beside me, flicked the mule with a switch and we set out for Mr. Arthur's farmhouse. It was sunny, a little cool this early in the day, and me and Mary were happy, I guess because Mama and Daddy seemed happy. Soon, we saw Mr. Arthur's place set back off the road. The wagon bumped down the driveway 'til Daddy stopped and tied the mule to a bush. While he headed around to the back of the house, we hopped down and followed, stopping there in the yard when Daddy walked to the back steps. Mr. Arthur came outside, told Daddy "Morning Jasper," and headed over to where he could lay his ledger on the side of the well. His wife pushed the screen door open with her foot and slung a pan of scraps toward a few chickens scratching around in the dirt. Mary squeezed my hand, and we stood still.

"You gals want to come get you a drink o'water?" she asked us.

"No'm, thank you," we told her, and she went back inside.

Daddy followed Mr. Arthur over to the well. He watched Mr. Arthur run his finger down the columns and turn the page. We couldn't make out what he was saying 'til he shut the ledger and told Daddy, "We had a pretty good year, Jasper, but I'm sorry, Jasper, there ain't nothing left. You done used it all up in credit."

"Now, Mr. Arthur. *Sir.*" Daddy says. "Must be some mistake in the figures. I been keeping track all along, and…"

But Mr. Arthur interrupts Daddy, "Now, Jasper, I've done gone over it and that's what it comes to. In fact, you went a little bit over, but I'm go' let that go. Prices went up at Reel's. Did you figure that in? We all go' do better next year."

"But Mr. Arthur, I got things wrote down, too, and my figures not the same as yours." Both of them quiet. Then Daddy speaks. "I think you wrong."

Mary and I tense up. We don't know what's gonna happen. But Mr. Arthur just kind of laughs and tells Daddy, "Jasper, you better check your figures again. You'll see I'm right. We'll do better next year, like I said." He reaches out to shake Daddy's hand, but Daddy just stands there looking at Mr. Arthur, then Mr. Arthur turns and heads back toward his house. Daddy still stands there. Finally, he comes and climbs back into the wagon. I hear him asking nobody, "How I'm go' tell Getsy there ain't nothing left? How I'm go' tell her that?" Me and Mary say nothing, just watch Daddy stare straight ahead. With the reins in one hand and a switch in the other, he struck the mule. He clenched his teeth with his lips parted. He turned the mule back toward home.

On our way back, the weather changed quick like it does sometimes in October down there. Clouds gathered and it started to rain, light at first, then a little harder, and the rain was cold.

Daddy pulled the wagon up under some trees to wait for it to let up. Rain dripped off the brim of his hat. When it slacked up, me and Mary climbed down to go relieve ourselves over in some weeds. Daddy told us, "Y'all watch where you step."

Mrs. Alexander, have you ever come up on something you never have seen before, but you know already that it's bad? That's what happened when we almost stepped on a yellow cat laying there in the weeds on its side with its legs sticking straight out. It looked like every bit of juice had been drained out of it. He was all sunk in – just bones and fur. His mouth was open, you could see his sharp, tiny teeth. His eyes were shriveled and sunk in, but open. Rain drops plopped into a little pool on his sunk-in body. And there's rope around his neck.

I bent down to look at it, but Mary pulled me back. "Get away from that, Carrie."

But I couldn't stop looking at it. "What you think happened to it? Can we help it?"

Daddy had got down from the wagon and come to see about us. He took ahold of my arm. "That cat is dead. Somebody mean done killed it. Ain't nothing we can do about that cat. Let's get back in the wagon." Daddy whipped the mule, and we jerked to a start, heading home.

My daddy prayed that night like he did every night before he went to bed. He always thanked God for Mama and us children, for a roof over our heads, and for God's son Jesus sent to save us. He asked God to help us get enough food to eat. I can see him on his knees, get up on one foot, then grunt while he stands up with the other foot, tired and stiff as he was at the end of every day. He always asked God to forgive him for his sins.

I never knew Daddy to do anything mean or hurtful to anybody. There wasn't but one time that I saw him get mad at Mama. We were at the supper table and Mama wasn't eating.

He asked her, "What's the matter, Getsy? You sick?"

She said, "Nothing. I'm all right."

Daddy got up from the table, went around to Mama and took her elbow and led her out on the porch. We watched and listened, frozen. He made her tell him.

"Webb." — that was the overseer. "When I finished my row and went to get water, he grabbed me and pulled me up next to him and reached his hand inside front of my dress."

Mama was crying a little by then. Daddy took hold of her elbow and said, "You look at him or something?"

She drew back a little and looked right up at Daddy. "*No!*"

He balled up his fist and hit the wall right close to Mama's face. Her head dropped down to the side like a flower on a broken stem. Daddy walked off down the road. Mama came back inside and sat down and laid her head on the table, her cheek against the cool wood. Mary wet a rag and pressed it to Mama's face and told her, "He didn't mean that. He knows you better than that. He just tired. He didn't mean it, Mama."

Daddy didn't come back in until after it had got dark, and we went to bed without talking. Why he got mad like that when it wasn't her fault I did not understand back then.

The letter came about Daddy when I'd been in Augusta for about five years. I was thirteen. It was from Mama's cousin Mrs. Hardy who lived next door to my family on Brooks Street. Aunt Lucy sat down at the table and held the letter in her hands a few minutes before she opened it. I was mending something. She read it to herself first. She looked at me, her eyes big and sad and her lips tight together, then took the sewing out my hands and pulled me over to her and down onto her lap, my feet touching the floor by then, and read me the letter.

> *February 13, 1923*
> *Dear Mrs. Oliphant,*
>
> *I am writing to tell you the sad news of the passing of Jasper Butler. Jasper and Getsy had been working in the field early in the morning when Jasper got to feeling sick and walked back to the house. The overseer let Getsy leave and when she got home, not long after Jasper, she found him on the floor. We believe he had a heart attack. The doctor wrote "old and worn out" on his death certificate. The funeral plan has not been set, but they're going to hold off on it until Carrie can get back home.*
>
>

Sincerely,
Frances Hardy

At first it didn't sink in. I asked Aunt Lucy, "What does that mean?" I buried my face in her dress and tried to breathe with her rocking and patting me. I kept trying to say, "That can't be right!" but I just croaked out noises while Aunt Lucy held me. That night I slept in her bed up next to her. I dreamed all night Daddy was alive and walking around, but I couldn't hear or feel him, and in my dreams, he kept falling.

The morning after that letter came, I woke up wondering if maybe I had just dreamed my daddy had died. I smelled biscuits cooking and sausage frying. I heard Aunt Lucy moving around downstairs. She came up carrying my church dress she had ironed and my good shoes, some that used to be Velma's. Her own church dress, a white linen shirtwaist with large buttons down the front, was hanging from the top of her bedroom door. She sat by me on the bed and hugged me and I knew it was not a dream. Lucy took me down and got me some breakfast, and one of her cousins showed up in his wagon to take us to Edgefield– me, Aunt Lucy, and my cousin Velma. Lucy told him, "We'll be ready in a minute. Come eat something while we finish up," then folded our church clothes and everything else we would take and placed them into a suitcase. She had packed a basket of sweet potatoes, greens, and apples that she set out to be loaded into the wagon, then went to Velma's room to tell her time to go.

That sad, fall feeling when the sun is shining through leaves that have turned red and yellow and brown, but still haven't all fallen off the trees was in the air that day. Velma wore a gray dress with a sweater draped around her shoulders. She rode on the seat with Aunt Lucy's cousin, and they talked some, but me and my aunt rode in the back with me leaning up against the front of her. On up in the morning, it got hot. The front of her dress and my own dress were damp, stuck to our skin. I kept my eyes closed and tried to just feel the bumpy road shake and jar us to keep myself from thinking. Light flashed on my eyelids as we rode in and out of shade. Once I got the image of Daddy coming in from the field and easing down in his chair to pull off his shoes — once I saw that in my mind, I couldn't stop crying.

The main thing I remember about my daddy's funeral is me and Mary holding Mama up — one of us on each side of her

— while we walked from the church out to the cemetery, stepping over rocks and weeds in the bright sun. Mama's arms felt bony, her hands were papery and cool. Fall in Edgefield can be hot or cold and this day started out warm, but by the time we got out in the cemetery, it had got chilly and you could smell wood smoke in the air. Mama was weak from the strain of the past few days, and she was also sick herself, but at that time, we didn't know just how sick she was. When we were about ready to leave the cemetery, she knelt down and scraped out a hole in the dirt on top of Daddy's grave, took Daddy's pipe out of her coat pocket, placed it in the hole, then patted dirt over it to help keep his spirit from wandering. She reached and got one of Mary's arms and one of mine and we lifted her up and walked her toward the wagon that her cousin Robert brought us in. Mama swayed a little bit, about to fall. Robert picked her up like she was a little child. The wagon creaked as he stepped up on the running board and set her on the seat. He smoothed her dress down around her legs, wrapped a blanket around her shoulders, and gave her his handkerchief. Me and Mary helped the other children into the back of the wagon, and he drove us back to our house late that afternoon. Both my little brothers clung on to Mary and whimpered off and on the whole way. Willis whined that he was hungry and Mary rocked him in her lap. Mattie and Mae just stared out the back of the wagon. I started to cry when I looked at Mama's back.

Chapter Three

FOR A WHILE AFTER DADDY DIED, MAMA COULD STILL WORK some in the field and she got a little money selling eggs, so that fall I went back to Augusta, excited to be in school again. I didn't get to stay long this time though. It wasn't long before my mother's kidney disease began to take a toll on her, and I had to go back home for good. It was like all of a sudden she was swollen and weak. Her back and side hurt her, and she itched all over. Seeing Mama so sick was hard. I wish she could have gone to a hospital, but hospitals didn't admit colored in Edgefield like they do here in Philadelphia. She never even set foot in a hospital but the one day when Daddy took her over to Augusta where she first got her diagnosis of kidney failure. Mary said when they got back from Augusta that night, after Mama got supper on the table and sat down, she started to say the blessing, but her voice caught in her throat — I guess the doctor had told her she was real sick by then. So, by late that year when my mother couldn't work at all, there was nothing to do but for me to go back home for good and help Mary take care of Mama and the other children, and work. By then there were four children younger than me — Mae, who was about ten when I went back; Mattie, who was eight; Willis, who would've been about six; and Jim, who wasn't but maybe four. My sister Mary was six years older than me.

Even if I could've stayed longer in Augusta, there wasn't a high school I could've gone to since Ware High School had been closed down. Ware had been the first public high school for colored in Georgia — Velma showed me where it was on the corner of Reynolds Street — but it closed because Georgia claimed it could educate colored children better if they spent all the funds on primary school. It went all the way to the Supreme Court to try to keep Ware open, but the colored lost. Aunt Lucy had wanted me to skip high school anyway and go on to Walker Baptist Institute, and I would have if I'd stayed on longer. She didn't want me to go back to Edgefield, telling me one time, "You lucky to be out of there. Lots of drinking and fighting. Folks there shoot each other over nothing."

Getting me ready to leave, Aunt Lucy washed and ironed all the dresses she'd made me and folded them up in a pillowcase for me to take home. Then she handed me a present wrapped up — a pair of scissors and a pack of sewing needles she had got free with a box of tea. She packed the scissors and those needles together with my slate I'd used at school, put all that in my pillowcase and fastened it.

Lucy's brother Thomas got there before daylight to take me home. He was a big man, gentle and soft spoken. He had a thick mustache that hung out far over his lip and down the sides of his mouth, and he wore overalls like Daddy. He had brought me a sack of pecans and after we got going, I cracked a few of them by squeezing two together between my hands until their shells broke open. Later I got so sleepy I leaned up against Thomas to keep from falling over when the wagon bumped. On up in the morning, it started misty raining, and the air was wet and cold. When the wind picked up, I turned my collar up close around my neck so it covered my ears because I'm easy to get the earache. Lucy had packed a bushel of sweet potatoes and wrapped up a slab of fatback for me to take home and biscuits and cheese for us to eat on the way. Thomas handed me his pocketknife to slice off some cheese, and when I handed the knife back, he told me, "You keep it. You might need it."

We'd been riding for hours, and I'd begun to drop my head when we hit a slick spot and one of the back wagon wheels slid off the road and mired up in mud. The mule strained to pull the wagon, but the wheel just wouldn't budge. I got out and pulled on the mule's reins while Thomas pushed on the stuck wheel. My shoes squished in the slick mud, and I felt them fill with water, so once we got going again, I took them off, and before long my bare feet went numb.

When we got into Edgefield, I saw wires attached to poles strung up everywhere — the new power lines that hadn't been there when I left. It was about dark, but coming down Brooks Street I could see the house the Morgans had lived in was burned out, the burnt smell strong in the cold, wet air. The whole way home I had pictured Mama come running out the door hollering and clapping her hands up at her chin and grabbing me and hugging me and taking me in and feeding me and standing me near the hearth to warm my feet. I expected to smell a wood fire and maybe some cornbread cooking. When we pulled up to our house in Old Buncombe — that's the section of Edgefield where colored people have lived since slavery — only Mary came out to meet us.

Thomas tied the mule up and handed me my pillowcase. He got the basket Aunt Lucy had sent and we followed Mary inside where it was nearly dark. The oil lamp burned low and only a few embers glowed in the fireplace. Mama was lying in her bed under several blankets. She was always pretty but her face was so swollen now, she didn't look like herself. She lifted her head a little to whisper, "Tunch, come over here to me, baby." Mary stood behind Mattie with her hands on Mattie's shoulders. Willis and Jim pulled on me, glad to see me, Willis telling me, "I'm hungry, sister. My belly hurts. Can we eat them potatoes you brought?" Mae put her arms around me and pressed her cheek on my chest and stood there with me, looking at Mama. I loosened them from myself, went over to Mama and climbed onto the bed and hugged her as easy as I could. She reached to fix her hair. She always kept it plaited neat but now it had come aloose and was matted in the back. I pulled it back from around her face and felt heat coming off her head. I could smell something bad in there that afternoon. You can smell it now, here in this ward. Its death, you know. Thomas still stood at the door, his hat folded under his arm. Mama spoke something to him, and he walked easy over to the bed and picked up her hand.

"How you doing, Getsy? Your baby girl about grown up while she was away. Lucy sent food for y'all." Thomas spoke to the other children then told Mama, "We all praying for you to get better, Getsy. You gonna get better soon. Anything we can do for y'all, you let us know."

Mama smiled, her eyes closed, and told him, "Thank you for bringing my baby home. Mary, get something for Thomas to eat and fix a place for him to sleep tonight. He can't start back and it dark."

He laid her hand down, looked silently over at us. Then Mary went to placing the potatoes Lucy had sent into the embers to cook for us to have for supper and making a pallet for Thomas to rest on 'til morning came and he could head back.

One night, Mama wanted us to find a leather pouch her grand-daddy had given her when she was a girl. "Will y'all get me that gunner's pouch? It's soft and smooth, about big as your hand. See can you find it." Mama's granddaddy had belonged to a soldier in the war who gave him that pouch. When the soldier got his leg blown off, Mama's granddaddy carried him into the woods and stayed with him while he died. But who knows where that pouch ended up. One thing she did have from way back was a piece of pottery that had been her mother's — a green clay jar about this tall. The man who made it belonged to the same man in Edgefield as Mama's grandfather. He had written a poem on that jar. I bet most his pots are gone now. You know how things get broke.

She talked about her own mother a lot during her last days. "Y'all never knew my mother. She had one brown eye and one blue eye, and she could see things with that blue eye other people couldn't see, like things going to happen, or somebody standing right there when that person might've been dead for years and couldn't nobody else see them." Near the end my mother said, "Mama's here." Mrs. Alexander, you think her own mother could've been there? Do you think when people are about to die that they connect with their folks who have already passed?

Last night here in the ward, something was disturbing everybody. Seem like everyone was restless, crying out and talking to people who weren't there. The night nurse stayed busy untangling bed sheets, pouring cups of water, shushing people to be quiet. Me, I had a dream about Mama's mother last night. She died before I was born, but I knew her in this dream. I was grown like I am now, and we were lying side by side on thick moss under a giant tree at the end of a long row of trees. The trunk was so big a grown man could not have reached around it and some of the branches were so twisted and heavy, they dipped down and touched the ground. The air all around us was cold, and when we breathed it in, it made us powerful. She looked up at the branches full of green leaves. I watched her blue eye swirl around like it had come undone.

She told me, "Somebody planted this tree a long time ago. You and me get to enjoy it, all those different greens, all this shade and beauty. Whoever planted it been dead a long time now. We born and die and after a while don't nobody know we were even here."

I told her, "But the tree's still here."

She patted my hand. "You right, baby. The tree is still here."

Every day toward the end our neighbor Mrs. Hardy brought us food and helped us feed and bathe Mama. She couldn't raise herself up on the bed, so Mary helped her sit up while I fed her. Just doing that little bit wore her out and she would lie back down and try to catch her breath. By then Mama wouldn't eat much of anything anyway. We had to get her onto the bed pan and sponge her off to cool her fever. Her arms and legs were thin, but her face and stomach were swollen. We each held one of her hands and talked with her. All I wanted was to make Mama feel better. She had seen a doctor that one time when Daddy took her to Augusta, but what medicine he gave her was long gone and it hadn't helped her much anyway.

Mrs. Hardy brought Mama some pennyroyal she'd made from a plant that smells like mint and tried to get her to chew on the root of a cotton plant, but neither one of those things did her any good. Every few days she took Mama's nightgown home and rinsed it out, and she took her blankets and hung them in the sun. Mrs. Hardy could read and write, something most women her age that I knew couldn't do. I wish I had asked her how she learned. One morning she read Mama a poem she herself had written just for our mother. She sat in the chair beside Mama's bed and read the Bible and prayed, holding Mama's hand. She always ended, "For God so loved the world that he gave his only begotten son that whosoever believeth in him shall not perish but have everlasting life." Mama did believe, and I think that gave her some comfort. Mrs. Hardy did so many things to make us feel better. Like one time she got some holly and some mistletoe her son had shot out of a tree with a slingshot, arranged it in the green clay jar, and set it on a table by Mama's bed.

Mrs. Hardy's son is kind like her. His name is Lewis. He got in trouble one time when he took a hammer from Reel's store, stuck it in his pants and pulled his shirt over it. He was just going to use it real fast and sneak it back in there, but Mr. Reel had been watching him and got in front of him so he couldn't leave the store. Lewis told Mr. Reel he was gonna bring it back soon as he used it to fix their roof, but Mr. Reel grabbed ahold of Lewis and told him "Lewis, you don't want to do this. Give me that hammer back and there won't be no trouble." When Lewis went to hand the hammer back to Mr. Reel, some men that had been standing around grabbed him and drug him to the sheriff's office, and said Lewis was about to attack Mr. Reel. But Mr. Reel wouldn't press charges, so they let Lewis go. My sister Mattie is married to Lewis now. That all seems like a million years ago. I wish I knew what it was like at the end for Mama — if she felt like she was drowning. I wish I could thank Mrs. Hardy for every kind thing she did for my mother.

———— ◆ ————

A new doctor made rounds in the ward this morning, but he didn't get around to me. My bed's the farthest from the door but it's close to the windows and that helps me get fresh air. It smells in here right now. There's somebody in all the beds today. Some lie there still, just looking like their eyes have died already. The new ones are restless and keep asking the nurse when they will see the doctor or if they can have water or something for pain. All day and all night I can hear the nurse telling someone, "Please be patient. You not the only one here."

You better rest now, Carrie. I've set a cup of water here by your bed. I'll be back again tomorrow.

Chapter Four

OH, MRS. ALEXANDER. I HOPE YOU HAVEN'T BEEN HERE LONG. I must have been asleep just now. I couldn't sleep last night for thinking about when I started to work at the Thurmonds'. I knew I would be telling you about that today.

My sister Mary got me that job. She had jobs working for different people over on Buncombe and Penn Streets, and she worked one day a week for Mister William Thurmond helping in the kitchen. The Thurmond family lived in a house on the corner of Penn and Bauskett Street on property big enough to have a farm back of their home. Besides Mary and their cook, Letha, they had another maid, a yard man, and a stoker who tended all their fireplaces. Letha would have breakfast ready, and the stoker would have the house warmed up before the family got up. Mary asked Letha if I could work there, too. I guess Letha got it OKed by Miss Eleanor Thurmond and in a few days, when Mary came home middle of the day — which she had to do to use the privy — she told me I could start to work there one day a week. I would get paid thirty-five cents a day to help Letha with things like peeling and chopping vegetables, setting and clearing the table, washing and drying dishes, sweeping, and taking out the garbage. With Mama so sick, and one of us needing to stay with her all the time, me and Mary tried to work opposite days if we could.

Right about then is when Mama was nearing the end. She would tell us she didn't hurt anywhere, but she was too weak to get out of the bed and she had got so swollen up by then that she didn't look like herself anymore — like me now some days. Her head hurt her most of the time — you could tell by how she would press her fingers to her forehead and squeeze her eyes shut. It was hard for her to breathe, and we'd roll a blanket up behind her to prop her up and that helped, but she had to work to take every breath. Mary would lift Mama's legs while I stuffed more pine straw into her bed to make it as soft as we could.

It was December and cold in Edgefield and we tried to keep a small fire going all the time. We had chopped most everything down around our house that we could burn, but every few days we'd hear scuffing and thumping noises outside the front door when one or another of our neighbors was leaving us some firewood on the porch. Most times it would be Mr. Magwood who owned the house we lived in and who stayed a few houses down the road from us. He had quit asking Mama for rent money after Daddy died.

With my mind on my mother, I also had to think about starting my new job. I was anxious, wondering if I could do everything right. Since Mary's day to work was different from mine, she wouldn't be there to help me. I was scared I'd do something wrong, break something, not know how to do what they wanted and get told to leave. To walk from my house on Brooks Street to where they lived took me a while, nearly half an hour. By then it was cold, and it was too hard for us to heat enough water to take a tub bath, and I started to worry that I might sweat and start to smell bad. With all those things gnawing at me, I had forgot I'd also have to worry about staying safe. Mary had been working as a maid long enough to know you had to be careful if you were alone with the husband — and sometimes the older sons — at some of the places where she worked. She started warning me about that as soon as I got my job.

"Keep moving and don't put yourself in any man's path if you can help it and don't get too close."

Then Mrs. Hardy warned me about the Thurmonds' youngest son, Strom. She knew things about him, knew that he liked girls, and they liked him. "He runs around town mornings taking exercise wearing nothing but short pants." Mrs. Hardy told me about a house over in Cleora not too far from Edgefield where two sisters lived, the Brunson sisters. They had colored girls they let stay upstairs and white boys could pay the sisters to go upstairs and be with one of the girls. Some of them were Christian boys from rich families — maybe not as rich as the Thurmonds — but Southern Baptists and Episcopalians, you know, prominent. Grown men went, too. A lady Mrs. Hardy knew whose daughter had got tangled up with the Brunsons told her someone looked a little like the youngest Thurmond boy went there. She told me, "Maybe him, maybe not. But that youngest boy's got big ambitions. He's been going to court to watch his daddy lawyering since he was big enough to sit still. You better watch out for him."

On the morning I was to start to work, Mrs. Hardy came over with some goat's milk she had boiled with dried parsley flakes and had me drink it while it was still warm. She said it would protect me from coming under the power of anyone who might want to harm me. With faith in Mrs. Hardy's knowledge of potions, I drank it all down and set out.

Walking to work, I thought about early mornings walking to school in Augusta with Velma. Our school was in the basement at the Tabernacle Baptist Church. To get to Tabernacle, we'd leave Aunt Lucy's early and head toward town, then cut through a vacant field to get to Gwinnett Street. If I wasn't careful not to let weeds brush up against me, my dress tail would be wet from dew and my socks covered in burrs and beggar lice time I got to the church. I thought about Velma and how she was probably reading over the lessons she had planned for her students, and I wished I was back walking to school in Augusta, with Daddy still alive and Mama well.

Instead of the Tabernacle Baptist Church in Augusta, Georgia, I was arriving at the Thurmond home in Edgefield, South Carolina, a two-story house with porches wrapped all around it sitting on a hill on about four acres of land. I stood at the bottom of the back steps until I got the nerve to go on up and knock. Letha must have been expecting me because she came and unlatched the screen door and just said, "Wipe your feet. You can help get breakfast to the table." Entering the back door was like stepping into a foreign land for me. First, I was hit with the smell of breakfast cooking. I worried I was going to track in dirt or grit onto those smooth, pine floors. It was too early for sunlight to be coming in, so the rooms were lit up with electric lamps and warmed by fires already burning in the fireplaces.

Once Letha had breakfast ready, Mrs. Thurmond came downstairs into the kitchen. She was wearing a dark dress and black lace-up, high-heel shoes. She wore a powder that smelled like dried roses. Letha took my elbow and presented me. "Miss Eleanor, this is Carrie. She's gonna be helping out in the kitchen like her sister Mary." First thing she did was hand me a white uniform dress and tell me, "I'm happy to meet you, Carrie. I hope you're as good a worker as your sister. Go in the storeroom and put this on. Wash it out every night and wear it every time you come. If you work out, I'll see you get another uniform so you can alternate them." I went and put the dress on over my clothes. It was short on me because I'm so tall but when I came out, she looked me over and said, "That will do." I stood and watched her run her finger around the inside of a pan that Letha had just washed. Letha got the coffee pot and followed her into the dining room. I picked up a dishrag and began wiping up around the dishpan.

Throughout that day, I moved from room to room, carrying things for Letha, bringing trays from the parlor into the kitchen, taking clean dishes into the dining room. In the parlor, besides the settees and chairs, were dark wood chests of drawers — five feet tall or more — with big, deep drawers and brass pulls. All over the walls were portraits of their kin looking stern and distinguished. Thick dark rugs covered the floors in the main rooms, and heavy drapes hung at the windows.

Most impressive of all to me was the dining room where a long, polished table was always set with china, all in matching patterns of birds and flowers, and polished silverware beside each plate. Cut flowers floated in a silver bowl in the center of the table. It looked like a place where a king could sit down to be served.

I would soon see that Mrs. Thurmond gave the family's morning devotional at the dining room table. She read from the Scriptures then prayed and thanked the Lord for their many blessings and asked him to bless them all that day and lead them not into temptation and forgive them their sins.

Who all lived there were Mister Will, Miss Eleanor, and their children: John William, Jr.; Alan, Strom, Gertrude, and the twin daughters, Martha and Mary. The two older sons were there some of the time. They had both been to medical school to be female doctors. Mister Strom had just graduated from Clemson College.

The family moved about in that house like it was nothing at all to be amazed by. I would not be stunned by it now that I've seen things here in Philadelphia, but I was awed by it back then. The house was obviously the home of powerful, wealthy people. In fact, Miss Eleanor's daddy was a doctor and a state legislator in the upper half of Edgefield, and Mr. Will's family was powerful in the lower half, so between those two families, they had influence all over the county.

Every time I got to work, before daylight, Letha would already be there. Letha was a small-built woman with smooth skin stretched tight on her face. I never knew how old. She kept her head down, but her eyes went side to side and took in everything. Letha had worked for the family long enough to know their likes and dislikes and did her job without talking much except to say "yes ma'am" to everything Miss Eleanor asked her to do.

One cold morning Miss Eleanor had a lady visiting who went to church with them. She told that her cousin's husband had a stroke and died. She said out loud, "I don't know how Mary Nell is going to get over losing her husband," then looked up at Letha who was pouring her more coffee and said, "Letha, you're lucky. You can just laugh your troubles away!" How she thought that about Letha I do not know. Letha turned her head away and shut her eyes. It hurt her to hear that.

The first time I met Mr. Strom, I was at the kitchen table cracking eggs into a big bowl for Letha to scramble once she had the bacon out of the pan. A tiny bit of eggshell dropped into the bowl, and I was trying to fish it out with a fork. Letha came over, picked up a piece of eggshell and used it to scoop out the broken piece. Soon as she did, she lifted it up to show me that's how you do it. I looked to the side and saw Mr. Strom standing at the stove, looking at the bacon Letha was frying. I noticed his high forehead and his eyes, how they're round at the corners. When he sees me looking at him, I'm startled and drop the fork I'm holding, and it clatters onto the floor. Mr. Strom turns, bends down and picks it up and hands it to me.

He's looking at me while he tells Letha, "Morning, Letha. I'm mighty hungry. I'll be in the dinin' room. And good mornin' to you, Miss."

"Mornin', Mr. Strom," Letha says, turning the bacon. "This is Carrie. She'll be helping out in the kitchen." His eyes scan my head to my feet then go back up to my face. I see Letha watch him look at me. He turns to go to the dining room, leaving the air smelling like shaving lotion and bacon swirled together. I take the fork and beat the eggs hard as I can.

I hadn't worked there but a few times before he would come in the kitchen and say things like "You look awful pretty today" or "You sure do have a pretty smile." He'd straighten the collar of my uniform, his fingers barely touching the back of my neck. Letha's back would go stiff. My own body would be paralyzed. I felt like he was always watching me. Even with your back to somebody you can feel their eyes on you. I breathed relief every time he left the house.

One day, I was standing at the counter washing dishes. Letha had gone out to the porch to shake crumbs off the tablecloth. Mister Strom came into the kitchen. He moved close to me, and I froze. He said, "Excuse me, Carrie," and reached from behind me to get something off a shelf and I felt him barely lean against my body. I didn't know what to do. I didn't move. Then he turned away and left the kitchen and I heard the front door open and close, and he was gone.

After that, when he came into the kitchen, I'd get behind the table or move a chair up behind myself and get busy like Mary had told me to do. But one day when Letha sent me to get sugar out the storeroom, I turned around and there he was, blocking me from getting out. I spilled the sugar. He stepped in close to me and said, "Morning, Carrie." He raised his eyebrows and smiled. He told me, "You very tall for a girl your age. You ought to be ashamed for being so pretty." I saw his shined leather shoes. He pulled me up against him. Then he leaned in and pressed me up against the shelves. I smelled his shaving lotion. He put his hand around my waist then moved it up and under my arm to where his hand was touching the side of my breast. Then someone was walking in the kitchen, so he let go and left. I wasn't able to move for a few seconds. I touched my breast like I have to see if it's still there. Then I smelled my hand and the shave lotion pricked the inside of my nostrils. Spilt sugar crunched beneath the soles of my shoes when I stepped to get the broom and dustpan. I caught a glimpse of Miss Eleanor's flowery dress passing in the hall.

Mister Strom had been hired to teach and coach all the sports over at the high school in McCormick, so he left out early. I had to be to work before daylight to help with breakfast, so he'd be in the kitchen time I got there. He began to take ahold of me and slide his hands over my waist and down my hips. I'd just stand still and shut my eyes 'til it was over. He was a grown man. I was just fifteen. Just a maid in the kitchen. I would *want* to say stop or push him away, but I wasn't able to do it. How *is* that? It was like in a dream when you try to yell and nothing will come out and you're paralyzed. I thought maybe every time would be the last time, but then the next time I worked, he would do those things again and I would just stand there while it happened. Two or three times I felt like his mama or one of the sisters had seen him messing with me, but if they did, they never said anything that I know of.

One morning Letha sent me to take linens upstairs right as Miss Eleanor and the sisters were leaving to go to a meeting at the First Baptist Church. I never had been upstairs before and where the doors were open, I could see into the bedrooms. I stood in the doorway and looked into Mister Will and Miss Eleanor's room. There was a little set of steps to climb up into the bed and fat pillows leaned up against the headboard. The fire had gone out in the fireplace but the room was still warm. Out the window I could see the peach orchard where workers were covering the trees with burlap to protect them from the freeze that was coming soon. I moved in just barely and saw Miss Eleanor's jewelry box with the lid open; I saw her ear bobs and pins, and a silver mirror and brush set on the dresser with her initials engraved onto them. Her powder was in a little tin with purple flowers on the front and a tiny green ball to lift the lid with. I reached to touch that little green ball. I wanted to smell the powder. Somebody's hand touched my arm from behind. I jumped back, then Mister Strom said, "What you doing up here, Carrie? Were you looking for me?"

I say, "No! No, sir. I came to put away laundry." I said, "I got to get back to the kitchen, Letha'll be looking for me," but he held my arm and walked me down the hall and into his own room where he eased the door to with the back of his foot. It was dark in there, still and cold, the bed made up tight and straight. There were books stacked up high on a desk. He drew me down onto the bed beside him. Next thing I knew, he was climbing over top of me and I felt his knee begin to push my legs apart. I lifted my head up to breathe. I felt his weight on me. Then all the sudden he was dead still. Somebody was coming upstairs. He got up and pulled me up and we stayed still and heard his daddy — that's who it was — walk around in the hall. He stopped outside the door, stood there still, then we heard him move away and go back down the stairs, then heard the front door open and shut. Mister Strom let out his breath then went out into the hall, and when he saw his daddy had gone, he came back in and told me, "Go back down to the kitchen." He put me out into the hall and closed the door from inside. My legs were trembling so hard, I had to hold to the banister to keep from falling down the stairs. I went back to the kitchen and found something to do quick, hoping I didn't look different when Letha came back in there

———◆———

Carrie, let me get you a little water or sponge your face off. Why don't you rest a few minutes before we go any further?

If you don't mind, I'm going to stop there, Mrs. Alexander. My pain medicine is wearing off and I need to turn onto my side. You'll come back tomorrow?

I will. I'll see you tomorrow.

Chapter Five

I WORKED AT THE THURMONDS' ONLY TWO OR THREE MORE TIMES before the day came that my mother died. Mary came up the back porch and when Letha answered the door, Mary asked her if I could leave a little early that evening since our mother was not doing well. Letha came in the kitchen and told me, "You need to get home, baby. Your mama's not doing well. I'll finish up."

Me and Mary hurried home. Mama had got to where she couldn't breathe hardly at all. Throughout that afternoon we tried to raise her up and get her to drink some water. When evening came, we got the children in their pallets where they settled down and fell asleep. I sat up with Mama all that night and Mary did, too. We kept the fire going since it was January and real cold that winter. I took deep breaths, willing her to breathe or trying to breathe for her while she gasped and wheezed, and sometimes we thought she had taken her last breath but then she would gasp in another rattling breath. Her eyes were half open, but they weren't seeing anything that was in that room. She talked a little, off and on, but we couldn't make out what she said. After midnight I heard her say, "Hold my hand, Mama." So I took her hand. Mary grabbed her coat and slipped out to go next door to get Mrs. Hardy. In just a minute, Mrs. Hardy came in quiet with some clean cloths and a pan of water. She sat beside Mama, dipped a cloth in the pan of water, wrung it out, wiped Mama's face and pressed the cool cloth on Mama's forehead. She dipped a corner in the water and squeezed it onto Mama's lips and Mama sucked at it like she was dying of thirst but most of it ran down the side of her chin. Right before daylight Mrs. Hardy went home just long enough to tell her son, Lewis, to go get Dr. Singleton. I went back and forth from Mama's bed to the window, watching for the doctor to come, but by the time he got there later that morning — January 6, 1925, — my mother, Getsy Weaver Butler, was gone. She was forty-five years old.

The next few days I watched Mary and my younger sisters move around silent, dazed. The boys did not understand and kept asking, "Where's Mama? When's she coming back?" And me, I couldn't think about anything but her struggling there at the end. I couldn't think past the next hour. Mrs. Hardy helped Mary make the funeral arrangements. Our neighbors brought in what food they could, maybe a half pone of cornbread or a few pieces of fried fatback. Mama's sister Bertha who lived on the other side of town from us came to help us clean up our house and see we had clean clothes to wear to the funeral. Then, a few days later, came time for the service.

It was freezing rain when we got to Mt. Canaan Baptist Church. I could feel people were inside the church when the family was walked in and sat down in front of Mama's open casket, but I never did look back at them. Mary had given Bertha one of the cotton dresses Aunt Lucy made me when I was in Augusta to take to the funeral home to put Mama in. It was yellow with a little blue flower. This time of year there weren't any real flowers to put in the church or on her grave, so I was glad she had those flowers on her dress. The undertaker had made her look beautiful and somehow got most of her swelling down. Her hair was oiled and smooth and her lips were colored a soft rose that made me think of Velma. I kept my eyes on my mother lying there and when they closed the lid on the coffin, I knew I would never see my mother again as long as I lived and maybe never to the end of time. Mae cried the most of all of us and I tried to hold on to her and keep her from shaking. Mattie held an arm around Willis and Jim. Reverend Willard Hightower, Sr., preached about how angels had come and taken Mama home and how she will not suffer anymore. That she is with Jasper and her own mother and father again and all her people who have gone home before her and she will never hurt or be sick or sad or hungry again. She is now in the arms of Jesus. I wanted to believe all that. I hoped so.

Outside at the grave, I saw somebody walking toward us through the grass and recognized Mama's sister Zula. She hadn't been at the service inside the church. For a minute, everyone was looking at Zula, her fitted black dress, her gloves and pocketbook. She came over to me, hugged me real hard, tears welled up in her eyes. Zula was tall and pretty, and when I was little, folks used to tell me I looked like her. Some of Mama's family had shut Zula out after she had a baby by one of their other sisters' husbands, but Mama had always stayed by her. Mama told us, "Who knows what the circumstances might've been. Judge not lest ye be judged."

There we were at our daddy's grave and there was the pile of red dirt they would use to cover Mama's coffin when they lowered her into the ground beside him. I had picked up Mama's piece of pottery, the only object besides her bible that meant anything to her, before we left the house that morning, and after Reverend Hightower prayed and the men from the mortuary began to shovel dirt onto her casket, I knelt and dropped it into the grave. Sleet had started coming down, and ice looked like rock salt began pelting the dirt covering her casket. One of the deacons from the church guided us away from the grave and to his wagon. By then sleet was coming down hard. We huddled under a tarp for the cold ride back home. Some of our neighbors — most of them our kinfolks — brought us food, walking it over throughout that cold, wet day, and some ladies Mama had gone to church with at Mt. Canaan did, too. We had more to eat than we had had in a long time.

Right after my mama died, I asked Mary how we were ever gonna pay for her funeral. Mary told me Mama had been paying twenty-five cents a month for years to the Mt. Canaan burial aid society for herself and Daddy so when their time came, they could be buried proper. Didn't matter how long you'd been paying, long as you had paid, the church found a way to take care of it. Thank goodness, because we didn't have any money. I been paying burial dues now myself to the church I go to here in Philadelphia.

———◆———

Carrie let's leave off here for the night. I have a long day in court tomorrow, but I'll come as soon as I can.

Chapter Six

I COULDN'T TAKE TIME OFF WITH SIX OF US TO FEED AND JUST ME and Mary who could work, so a few days after my mother's funeral, I went back to work.

Walking there cold, it still dark out, I'd think about when she and Daddy both were alive and Mama wasn't so sick, and how they used to get up before daylight for Daddy to get a fire going and Mama to get everybody's breakfast laid out, usually molasses on a piece of bread. I'd see Daddy hitching his overalls up onto his shoulders and sitting down to pull on his heavy shoes and Mama on the side of their bed, her fingers working like spider legs, plaiting her hair and twisting the ends up under the plaits, the room smelling like woodsmoke and bread, and me, still, under a quilt on the pallet up next to Mary who was always warm. Why couldn't they still be there is all I could think about. I wished so bad if I could just see them one more time.

It was end of January. Mama had been dead two weeks, maybe not even that long, when Mister Strom came in the kitchen after breakfast and told me, "I understand that your mother passed away recently. Is there anything our family can do for you? I'd be happy to contribute something if there was a funeral fund." I looked to Letha who looked away.

I told him, "Thank you. My mother paid into a fund at her church that took care of everything."

"I'm sure we could offer you some vegetables that will keep awhile for you and your family. I'll see that some of those get packed up for you to take home."

The next day Mister Strom came into the kitchen when I was in there by myself. He told me again that his family would like to provide some things we could eat on for a while. He said, "I see no one has packed up some food for you to take home, but we can take care of that now." He put his arm around me and told me he was sorry about my mother passing. Then he told me to come with him to the shed outside and he'd help me gather up anything I thought we could use. He took my elbow and walked me outside.

Going through the yard down to that building, I was so uneasy. I was very uncomfortable, but it was awfully kind of him to offer me the food. You know we never had enough. I didn't want to seem ungrateful. I couldn't say to him, "You go get it; I'll wait here." You know what I mean, Mrs. Alexander? I had to go with him to be polite.

When we got down to the shed, he turned the wooden block and the door swung out. He helped me inside then stepped in close behind me, pulled the door to and tied it shut with a piece of rope, to keep it warmer in there, he said. Barely any light came through gaps between the wall boards, and it was so cold in there, I could see my breath. I was shivering from the cold, so he took his jacket off and draped it around my shoulders. I smelled bacon grease in his wool coat mixed with that spicy shave lotion I had smelled before whenever I was near him. An odor was coming off me, too — something like metal. I can smell it all now.

Very quietly, he told me, "You look mighty pretty today." He leaned in to me and my head started to spin. He began to rub my back with both his hands. *In my mind,* I was thinking, "Please don't get so close! Please stop!" But I was paralyzed and no sound came out of my throat. Things happened. It's so hard to remember. Time stopped and my mind stopped registering anything. I remember him wiping himself off with his handkerchief and then handing the handkerchief to me. I remember staring at it in my hand. Then he looked through a crack between the boards to see if anyone was out there. He told me, "Wait a few minutes before you come out." He smoothed his hair and checked his clothes again and told me, "You get on back up to the house soon as I get gone," and he was out the door.

I leaned headfirst against the wall. I tried to get my breath. I looked down and saw drops by my feet, black drops against the dark wooden floor. Is that my *blood?* I used the handkerchief to wipe the blood between my legs, then folded it and put it inside my drawers. I cracked the door and saw his car was gone and that it had started snowing. I moved toward the house. Snowflakes stuck to my face as I walked back through the yard, crossing over tracks he made in the light covering of snow. The wind stopped blowing and everything was still and quiet the way it gets when snow starts to fall.

Back inside, the warm kitchen still smelled like bacon. Letha didn't look up from the pan where she was washing breakfast dishes. She told me, "There's potatoes needs to be peeled. You can sit here and do that while I take the garbage out." I saw dried blood on my leg and stood to one side where Letha couldn't see it, then spit on my fingers and rubbed it off. After supper that night, Letha wrapped all the leftovers from dinner in a pan and handed it to me and told me she would get the kitchen shut down and for me to go on home.

Walking home, I was hurting and stinging. Snow had turned to freezing rain that was covering the road in a slippery glaze. Tiny pieces of ice pinged against my face, but the pain felt good. Once I could see our house, just barely lit, I started running. The asphalt road ended, and I was on the dirt road that was Brooks Street. My shoe caught on a tree root that ruptured the ground and slammed me down on the road. The side of my head hit hard in the mud. I cut my lip. The rest of the way, my teeth crunched dirt and I spit out dirt and blood. Soon as I walked in the door, Mary knew something was wrong. She sent the other children to bed and hung up the blanket to section off the room. There was no light except light from the fire. Mae pushed the blanket back a little to see what was happening. Her chin dropped down to her chest like it always did when she felt pain — hers or anybody else's. By then I was sobbing. I tore my dress getting it off. Mary took the blanket off our bed and wrapped it around me, then wrapped her arms tight around the blanket to get me to stop shivering. She heated water on the fire and wet a rag to clean off my face. She brushed a pinch of ash away from the fire and when it cooled, pressed it into the cut on my lip.

We just stared into the fire. We didn't speak. When Mary bent over to get my dress, I took the bloody handkerchief off of me and threw it to the fire, but Mary told me, "No!", grabbed the poker and raked it out of the fire.

"No! Burn it! I don't even want to touch it. We not washing that out!"

"Wait, don't burn it. It's something I heard from Bertha we can do with it. It's a way to make a man weak, make him not be able to do what he did to you no more. See, this what Bertha told me. If a man is treating a woman bad then has relations with her, she can take a rag they both used to clean theirselves with, tie seven knots in it, then throw it in the river. Then he ain't able to have relations anymore unless she gets the rag back out of the water and unties the knots. So, we gonna take this handkerchief, and we tie seven knots it. Then we gonna weigh it down with a rock and throw it in a creek. He won't be able to do nothing to you no more."

"Where we gonna drop this in any creek?"

"I'm gonna do it. It's going to the bottom of Beaverdam Creek. Don't ask me how, but it's going in there tomorrow. Bertha'll help me."

So, I watched Mary there by the hearth, her dark skin glowing and flames reflecting in her eyes, knotting the handkerchief, her head bowed. Looked like she was praying on each knot. I tell Mary, "I can't go back! We got to find me somewhere else to work! Please, Mary!" She didn't say it, but I knew. I got to go back. Until I can find other work. We got to eat. How would I go back there? But I would have to sew up my uniform where I tore it and rinse it out so I could wear it to work next time I went.

I laid in our mother's bed with Mary all that night half awake, still burning and stinging, and she held me in her arms like I was a child.

———◆———

Mrs. Alexander, that's how it happened. That's how I got pregnant with Essie Mae.

Carrie, why didn't you tell someone when this happened to you? Someone besides your sister.

Mrs. Alexander, who could I have told?

Chapter Seven

After Mama died, I counted on Mary for everything. She was working, she got me work, she got us all fed — five of us younger than her. We helped, but she was taking up where Mama and Daddy had been. She was all I had for comfort and protection. But soon she was gonna be gone, too.

Mary had started talking to a man we had always known — he lived in Old Buncombe, too — named John Washington. John was getting letters from his cousin who had gone north to Coatesville — that's about thirty miles from here in Philadelphia — and got a job in the Lukens Steel Mill. They supply most of the steel for US Navy ships and big bridges. This was a regular-paying job. Kind of job a man couldn't get in Edgefield. His cousin said John could get a job there, too, and John was determined to go and wanted Mary to go with him. The thing that pushed him over the edge to leave was when he got chased one night all the way from a farm where he had been picking cotton, to his sister's house in Old Buncombe by a gang of white men who were riled up about a colored boy who had refused to pick up a rake that the overseer threw at him. The boy had run off and hadn't been found, and some white men in the town were just ready to get after any colored man they could find. John's sister let him in, and he hid at her house all night. The next day he showed up early at our house knocking at the door. Mary let him in. He told Mary, "I'm going North, and you can come with me or not. Please, Mary, I want you to. I hope you do, but I have got to leave here."

I heard Mary whisper to him, "I will go if we get married first."

When Mary told me her plans to marry John Washington and move to Coatesville, I didn't see how I could stand it. I told her, "You can't go, Mary. I can't do it all by myself." I didn't tell Mary I had not bled since the day in that shed, right after Mama had died. I was too terrified to let myself think what it must mean, much less tell it out loud to someone else.

"You won't have to stay here much longer. When I get North with John and can send the money, all y'all can come up there, too. Come on, Tunch, this might be only chance I have to get married and to get out of here. Please don't ask me not to do it."

So, John got the money together to buy train tickets for both of them, and they got married a few days later on a Sunday. All of us went to church that day — us girls wearing one of the dresses my Aunt Lucy had made me, mine and Mary's too short and too tight, and Mattie's and Mae's hanging loose on their little frames. Jim and Willis wore what clothes they had, but neither one of them had shoes. We walked to Mt. Canaan and after the regular service, Reverend Vaughn married Mary and John there in the church. He ended with "'til death do you part."

The next morning, John's brother took them to the Southern Railroad Depot. They hadn't told many people they were leaving because so many colored people were leaving to go North that white bosses down there were making it hard for colored workers to get away, scared there wouldn't be enough colored left to work the fields. The morning they left, she told me again, "Things going to be better up there and y'all coming as soon as we get settled. Just hang on for a while. Just take care of yourself." She asked me in private, "You doing all right?" I know she must have been wondering about the night of what happened to me, wondering if it had made me pregnant, wanting assurance that wasn't the case. I told her, "Yeah, I'm all right."

I rode with them to the train where John broke me and Mary apart so they could board before something happened to keep them from going. Now Mary was gone, Daddy and Mama gone, and soon my little brothers, Willis and Jim, would be gone.

Here's how that happened. Not long after Mary left, Daddy's cousin Nathaniel Hughes and his wife, Viola, from over in Trenton came to see us one day and brought us a sack of potatoes and turnips and talked to me about taking Willis and Jim to live with them. It was strange to think about letting my little brothers go live with someone else — someone we barely knew even though they were our kin. The last time we had seen them was the summer before I left for Augusta when they came to see us with their son, Paul, who was my age. Paul brought a pouch of marbles and taught us how to shoot marbles out in the yard that day. Then Paul died right before Christmas that winter from influenza. Viola's eyes got wet and soft when she looked at Willis and Jim. I guess they made her think about Paul. Nathaniel said he needed the boys to help him on his place and that it would help us, too, since we were having a hard time feeding us all. Viola gave a little pouch of marbles to Willis and Jim — I knew those must have belonged to Paul — and gave all of us a peppermint. She tempted them with things she had to offer, hoping they would want to go. "We have a pretty little dog name Crystal y'all can play with. My sister Addie and her husband, Joe, live down the road from us and Joe works for the railroad. He might can get y'all a ride on a train!" Nathaniel said they'd be back in a few days to see what we had decided. After the boys went to sleep, I asked Mattie and Mae, "What y'all think we should do?" Now that Mary was gone, I was the oldest and the one to make the decision.

Mae didn't want them to go. She pleaded with me not to let them go. "They'll be OK here with us. I'll take care of them. I take care of them now! You'll get more work. We can grow more food." Mae was always tenderhearted and gentle, and it had been Mae that held them at night to go to sleep after Mama died. Mattie, though, she knew like me that it would be best for all of us if Nathaniel and Viola took Willis and Jim. Our brothers were still young, and it would almost be like they had a mother and father again. They would be more likely to have plenty to eat. I was just barely fifteen. I knew if they left, it would take some of the burden off the rest of us. And it would help Nathaniel and Viola, too. And I think Mama would have thought it was for the best. I did not want to hurt Mae, or Willis and Jim, but I made the decision to let them go.

I packed up what clothes the boys had — just some raggedy britches and some shirts that Mattie and Mae had outgrown — they still didn't have any shoes. Nathaniel and Viola came back in a few days like they said they would and eased Willis and Jim into going with them. Viola put an arm around each one and started walking them to the wagon telling them, "You fellas coming with us for a while. It's go' be good," as she looked back at me, and they both started crying — Jim was still crying for Mama some days, but as Viola led him away, he was crying, "I want Mae. I want to stay with Mae." Mae stood there, her arms around herself, tears trickling down her face.

I can still see Jim's thin arm up over his head as Viola held his hand and walked him toward the wagon. I ran and helped him climb into the wagon and told him, "We'll come see y'all soon." I hugged them both hard. Nathaniel told me, "They'll be like our own" as Viola climbed in after Jim, and Nathaniel clicked his tongue at the mule, and they pulled away, Jim and Willis looking back and Viola putting an arm around each one and trying to turn them in the direction of the mule.

I haven't ever seen them since, and I guess I won't now. Some time back we got word that Nathaniel died, and our brothers went North to work when they got old enough to leave. The last I heard, they were in Chicago, and they had sent money for Viola to come up there. She must be at least sixty by now. That left Mae and Mattie and me. We went back in the house and just laid on the bed and said nothing while it grew dark.

————◦————

As far as surviving — I don't know how we would have got by if our neighbors hadn't helped us and brought us food when they could. It might have been a turnip, two or three eggs, or part of a loaf of bread, but we were glad to get anything. Everybody on Brooks Street was hungry like us. I was working two or three days a week now and most nights I brought home leftover food that Miss Eleanor told Letha and me we could have, but for the three of us, we never had enough. We went to bed with our stomachs rumbling and woke up with our stomachs rumbling. I had never felt so hungry in my life. I was getting big, and I was terrified of what that meant.

Chapter Eight

Strom was still teaching in McCormick. I heard him tell his family at dinner how well the football team was doing with him as coach — still losing but doing a lot better than last year. "Folks 'round McCormick are congratulatin' me," he told them. "Givin' me advice," he laughed. He told them he had sent a letter to the McCormick newspaper offering to teach adults to read if they hadn't had a chance to get any education.

I was working more days now that Mary had married John and gone North, but Mr. Strom wasn't coming after me as often, which was a small relief. The family had dinner every night in that big dining room with the china and silverware. I helped carry in steaming serving dishes and pour glasses full of tea or water. I helped Letha go back and forth into the kitchen throughout the meal, keeping everybody served. We kept the candles lit if Miss Eleanor wanted candles instead of the electric lights and we raised or lowered the windows depending on if she was hot or cool. They would have three or four different vegetables every night — like peas, corn, green beans, butterbeans, collards, turnips, potatoes, tomatoes — always bread, sometimes biscuits, sometimes cornbread, maybe whole-wheat bread made from grain they grew. And meat — beef or chicken, sometimes ham or pork roasts. We cooked dessert about every night, too, whether it was a cake, or a peach pie out of peaches Letha had put up in the summer. It was more food than you could imagine every night and I had helped cook or peel or stir or fry or pat out most of it.

After dinner, we served the coffee — to all except Mr. Strom who didn't take coffee — while they talked and laughed and argued. I helped Letha carry all the cups and saucers, dishes and bowls back into the kitchen after they were through and scrape them off into the garbage. Sometimes I popped bites of food they'd left on their plates into my mouth. Letha did that, too. Miss Eleanor almost always came in the kitchen after dinner and told us if there was food left over, we could take home a service pan — that was what she called a pan of leftovers. Letha made up the pans for us and usually gave me more than she took for herself. Then we washed and dried glasses, dishes, silverware and pots and pans — in that order the way Miss Eleanor said to — for an hour at least, and I took out the garbage and swept the floor and we got everything put away and the kitchen closed up and then we could both go home. Mae and Mattie would be watching for me, waiting to see what I had brought back for us to eat.

Letha had a grown daughter named Callie who wasn't all there. She had light-colored skin — almost yellow — and green eyes. She didn't look like she could have weighed more than eighty pounds. When Letha did talk a little to me about something besides work, it was usually about Callie, about leaving her by herself all day, afraid she might go out and get lost or light a lamp and get burnt or set the house on fire and not be able to get out. We worked fast after dinner so we could get home, but it was a hard job getting all those dishes washed and put away and the kitchen closed for the night. Most nights it was dark time we left.

While we cleaned up, the family would move over to the parlor and listen to records or read the Bible and talk about things that were happening around Edgefield, all over South Carolina, and all over the country. A lot of times Mister Will had people there for dinner and they would get to talking heated and loud about news and politics and other people. They talked about everything under the sun from crop prices, a monkey trial in Tennessee, white Christian America, the Ku Klux Klan marching in Washington, and prohibition. I wanted to know about all those things, especially the monkey trial. I wanted to read and learn about all of it, but the way we lived, events in the world didn't get through. I thought of Velma and how she kept up with news and wished I still had that link to the outside world. Mister Will and his friends would still be going strong when I left out the back door to go home where it was quiet and dark.

I think Mister Will would have been in politics — he ran for Congress one time and lost — but he had shot and killed a man right outside his law office and that kept Mister Will from running again. People who saw it happen said Mister Willie Harris was drunk and started arguing with Mister Will, calling him a low-life scoundrel, so Mister Will pulled out a gun and shot him in the chest. Then at his trial for murder, Mister Will claimed he shot Willie Harris in self-defense. He got off.

———— ✦ ————

That doesn't surprise me, Carrie. Not considering who he was. Here's the nurse with your medicines. You better rest. I'll see you tomorrow.

Chapter Nine

FOR WEEKS ON END I WOULD PRAY, "PLEASE, GOD, LET ME START bleeding again. Let this be a bad dream." But it was no dream. I kept getting bigger. My white uniform fit tight around my ribcage and gaped open down the front between the buttons. When Miss Eleanor or any of the sisters came into the kitchen, I kept my back to them if I could or held a plate or tray in front of me. When I saw Letha looking at me one day, I knew she knew. Her eyes dropped down to my belly, her lips pressed tight together, then she looked back up at me. She looked angry. My face went hot. I crossed my arms to cover my belly. I felt ashamed. Now, years later, I think about Callie and her yellow skin and green eyes, and I believe what happened to me had happened somewhere to Letha. I try to see Letha's face in my memory. Maybe it wasn't anger. Or maybe it wasn't anger at me.

One of the Thurmond sisters, Miss Martha, began to treat me different, kinder. She had a soft voice, just moved and spoke so gentle. While Letha and I got the kitchen shut down after dinner, she often came in and packed up more leftovers for us to take home — even if Miss Eleanor had already told us we could fix a service pan. Maybe she noticed I was getting big. Maybe she knew things. I don't know.

But the one I was most scared of noticing me was Mister Will. I can still see Mr. Will — his broad forehead, big dark eyebrows, and tight mustache. But what made me afraid of him was the way you could feel he was in charge. He didn't talk down to people, he didn't talk loud, but he said everything stern and looked you in the eye, without explaining anything, and nobody questioned what he said. Same with how he walked — straight ahead with his eye set on where he was headed. I was afraid he would fire me if he knew, and who knows what else he could do to me. I have to tell you he did do good things for lots of folks in Edgefield whether white or colored, rich or poor. He had many times got me and Letha to pack up food for him to take folks in town who had had a death in the family. He often thanked Letha, and sometimes me, for things we did, and he never spoke harsh to us. I heard him one morning in the dining room tell Mister Strom, "Don't ever miss an opportunity to help somebody if you can, son. You never know when you might need them to do something for you. And *always* do what you say you will do." Mister Strom told him, "Daddy, if I give somebody my word, I swear to you I will keep it."

I remember that day, Mrs. Alexander. That's why I told you I think Strom will keep his promise about Essie Mae going to college.

All the Thurmond children looked up to Mr. Will and did whatever he said do — especially Mister Strom. Mister Will had power over everybody. My mouth went dry, and I would break out in a sweat every time I had to be in the same room with him.

During that time my mind got separated from my body. I kept getting bigger. I kept needing to get food to Mae and Mattie and for myself and my baby, too. I was so scared; I was nearly paralyzed. We all stayed hungry. The food I brought home on the nights I worked allowed us to sleep without our stomachs churning but on the days I didn't work we had to get by on so little. I don't know how I stayed up on my two feet to go to work and do what I had to do every day. Right there in that house I could see him and his family still living their regular lives like nothing had changed, while I was so distracted I couldn't hear anything but wind in my head. I still remained silent and unable to move any time Strom came at me. One time I had the thought that he might have started to care about me, but I knew better. Then he suddenly stopped coming at me altogether, avoided me it seemed like. I got so scared and confused and worried that the thought of being dead slipped into my mind, how I wouldn't have to worry about anything ever again. But who would have taken care of Mattie and Mae?

Going to work during that time, I was in a fog or a dream. I knew I was pregnant, but my baby didn't seem real yet. Not until the night of Mr. Strom's dinner party for his basketball teams. The morning of the party, I got to work when Miss Eleanor was telling Letha that Mister Strom's McCormick basketball teams — boys and girls — were playing the Edgefield teams that afternoon, and that he had invited the McCormick players to come home with him after the games to have dinner. The party was even written up a few days later in *The Edgefield Advertiser*. Every detail of that evening has stayed clear in my mind.

Miss Eleanor was busy getting the dinner menu decided on and making sure the house would be gleaming clean and that the yard man knew to get the front yard trimmed up and flowers cut to fill up the vases and the silver bowl. She was examining everything close and checking things off her list with a pencil. With all we had to do, Letha offered to go home and get her daughter, Callie, so she could help, too. Miss Eleanor told her, "Yes, go get her." It crossed my mind to offer to get Mattie or Mae to help, but I put that thought out of my head. I didn't want either of them to wade into that situation for fear of what it might lead to. But it was a good thing that Callie came. She helped string beans and shuck corn and ironed the napkins and the tablecloth while we cooked. We spent the day cleaning, peeling and chopping, baking, setting the table, and checking the glasses for spots. I had started getting sick in the mornings by then and it was all I could do not to be sick smelling the food cooking and at the same time feeling hungry. Miss Eleanor had one of the other maids polishing silver and had me get out all the extra serving pieces she used on special occasions. She told me to climb up on a stepladder to get a heavy silver tray off the top shelf of the cupboard and soon as I got ahold of it, I got dizzy and fell off with the tray in my hands. I landed on my bottom and the tray clanged and bounced and slid across the floor. Letha hurried over to see about me. Miss Eleanor rushed over to me, too, and took my hand to help me up. Her touch was startling. I moved to pick up the tray, afraid it had got dented or scratched, but Miss Eleanor steadied me and held my arm while Letha picked up the tray. After a minute, I got back to work and in a little while I felt cramping in my stomach. I thought maybe the fall had jarred the baby loose and I would lose it. I don't know if I was scared that would happen or hoping that it would. A couple of times Letha whispered, "You doin' OK?" as we kept on working. Once, she put her hand on my back and patted me a little, the most I ever knew her to be gentle like that.

It took us all day to get everything ready, and finally we heard cars driving up to the house — Mister Strom with his car full of children and then a few of the boys driving their families' cars with three or four boys and girls in each one. Letha and I looked out the window and saw all those children jump out and come up the steps onto the porch with Mr. Strom in the lead, them looking all around and into the lit-up house. They were talking and laughing, moving quickly up the steps, all shiny and smiling.

I guess they had changed out of their basketball uniforms at the school before they left. Now they had on Sunday clothes and shoes and the boys had combed their hair down and the girls had put on dresses and brushed their long, shiny hair, or clamped it over to the side or tied it up with a ribbon. Letha and I began to get the food going into the dining room while those children whispered and giggled and said "yes ma'am" and "yes sir" and looked around, taking it all in like I did the first time I was in there. They stood in the hallway being introduced to Miss Eleanor who smiled and hung out her hand to welcome each one of them while Mr. Strom introduced them to her, then they moved on into the parlor where Miss Eleanor had had us set out little dishes of divinity candy and cheese wafers.

From the kitchen I heard Mister Strom pointing out those portraits of his kin who did famous things and Revolutionary War guns mounted on the wall and things like that. I heard one of the boys ask Mister Strom, "Was your daddy in the Revolutionary

War?" and I wondered if he was bad at arithmetic or history, or if he couldn't think right because he was just nervous. Then Miss Eleanor clapped her hands and said, "Would everyone please join me in the dining room!" She had set out little cards with their names written on them so they would know where to sit and had them sitting boy girl, boy girl all the way down the table with Mister Strom at one end and herself at the other.

Two pretty girls were seated at Mr. Strom's end of the table — one on each side of him. Those two couldn't take their eyes off him except to look down at their laps and giggle, and he couldn't keep his eyes — or his hands — off them either. He scooted the chair up for one and touched her shoulders, then walked around and did the same for the other one. At his seat, he leaned into each one when she spoke. He seemed to like the smaller one best. She had long, smooth hair and deep-set blue eyes with long black eyelashes. Her dress was pale blue with a cream-colored lace around the neck and down the front to the waist and around the bottom of the puffy sleeves. It was made out of something fluffy, maybe chiffon. He told them all, "Let's join hands and bow our heads. Mrs. Thurmond will return thanks."

Miss Eleanor prayed, "Our Heavenly Father, we ask that you bless this food to the nourishment of our bodies. Bless each one here and be with them and protect them during their basketball games and into the future as they continue their education. We thank you for all our many blessings and ask that you lead us not into temptation. Forgive us our many sins, Lord. In Jesus' name we pray. Amen." Strom held those girls' hands the whole time while they bowed their heads and shut their eyes and smiled. Letha and I started setting down the plates of fried chicken and the bowls of gravy and green beans and potatoes and corn and the breads in the center of the table, and then we brought in the tea pitchers and the cakes and pies and placed them on the sideboard. The children were awkward about how to pass the bowls of food, and I cringed when I heard Miss Eleanor's china bowls click together. They were my same age and were going to high school and it hurt me to think of what all they could learn, and it hurt to think I wouldn't get to go to school any more. Some of them would go to college, too. I wondered if they knew how lucky they were.

Back in Augusta, I had wanted to follow in my teacher Velma's footsteps. She graduated from Atlanta University and started teaching when she wasn't but twenty years old. I learned about so many different things back there — the pyramids and pharaohs in Egypt, mummies, the Middle Ages, the Renaissance, the French Revolution, about George Washington and Abraham Lincoln, about a man who believed the continents of the world had once been joined together with no ocean separating them. Velma told us a scientist had discovered the earth was over two billion years old. She read us about Amelia Earhart and Charles Lindbergh. She taught us about colored people who had done famous things like Madam C.J. Walker who invented cosmetics for colored women and a man named Morgan who invented gas masks that saved soldiers' lives in World War I. And who knew that the first person to reach the North Pole was a colored man? I should remember his name. Some days, though, Velma just read stories to us. I loved when she read us *National Velvet*. I knew that, since this was just a book, when Velvet Brown prayed to be the best rider in all of England, God would answer her prayer. The children at that dinner would not have believed I knew about anything more than cooking and cleaning. They'd probably be surprised I could add two plus two.

They were all enjoying that evening, even the ones who were unsure about which fork to use, and which glass was theirs. The air was vibrating, glasses and silverware were tinkling, candles were glowing, and the flowers were putting out sweet and beautiful smells. All the children were excited, almost giddy, the boys clearly trying to be polite and use their best manners but enjoying the good food, the girls mostly just nibbling at it. One boy asked Mister Strom about his college classes at Clemson, announcing that his own daddy planned to send him there. Strom described some of his classes and a couple of his professors, then told them about two men from South Carolina who had connections to Clemson — John C. Calhoun who donated the property Clemson was built on, and Pitchfork Ben Tillman who nearly beat a Northern man to death with his cane on the floor of the United States Senate for insulting the South. Tillman, he told them, was one of his daddy's heroes. Later Mr. Strom threw out questions like "Who is your hero?" or "What do you want to be when you grow up?" and went around the table letting them answer, making generous and approving comments about each one. All of them had hopes and dreams. I thought about Velma and all the things I had learned from her and wondered if these boys and girls had heard about any of those same things. I wondered what it would be like to be white.

One of the pretty girls seated next to Mr. Strom — the one he kept his eyes on the most — was stammering a little answering her question. She swallowed something the wrong way and Mister Strom quickly held her glass of tea to her lips and put his other hand to her back. She took a big sip, coughed, and spurted tea out onto her dress, and when she grabbed for her napkin, she knocked the glass of tea out of his hand, and it spilled on her dress and the floor. She jumped up to clean up the tea, but Strom rose half way up out of his seat and pressed her back down with his hand on her shoulder. He is calm. He tells her, "Sit still, honey. You just sit still, sweetheart — the girl will clean that up," and without even looking at me, "Run get Miss Johnson another napkin, Carrie, and hurry and get this up off the floor."

Then the girl herself, looking down at her lap, worried about her dress and aiming her voice in my direction yelled, "Hurry!"

I rush to the kitchen and grab a napkin and some clean rags. My teeth are chattering, and as I cross the threshold going back into the dining room, I feel something bump and flutter inside me. It stuns me for a second. I stand still. My baby. The first time I felt it move.

Then both of them telling me, "Hurry!"

I can't remember anything that happened that night after that.

Chapter Ten

I DON'T KNOW WHEN THE FAMILY KNEW THAT I WAS GOING TO have a baby, but I sensed that they did. All of them. When one of them came into the kitchen, when I carried plates to the dining room, when I was sweeping the hallway, I could feel their stares. I'm sure they wanted to see that my belly was not big after all, that they had been mistaken to think I was swollen, that maybe their eyes had looked at me wrong. One day something happened that told me my instincts were right — Mister Will was blocking the kitchen doorway when I got to work that morning, standing with a folded newspaper in his hand. As I was walking slow toward the kitchen, he locked eyes with me. He tossed the newspaper toward a table, and it fell onto the floor in a mess of pages, then he walked out the kitchen, brushing past me so close I felt the air between us move, and then he was out the front door.

I didn't know what he was about to do but I feared it was something bad for me. What did he know about my baby? Should

I run home and never come back? I was afraid to stay there and afraid to leave. But my body was chained down. There was Mattie and Mae. Mary was gone. Mama and Daddy were gone forever. In my time with Aunt Lucy in Augusta I was somebody who could decide to do things, but not here. There I had been somebody learning about geography and explorers and clouds and layers of the earth and grammar rules. All kinds of things. And imagining what it would be like to go to college and making plans. Now, here, I couldn't decide anything for myself. I had lost control of my own body like it was not mine anymore. I felt like I was welded to this family. To this house and these people. To Mr. Strom. My mind had been fractured. You can't understand how powerless I felt. But the night of the party when I felt my baby move, my instinct to protect her began to outweigh my fear.

Do you remember the Brunson sisters I told you about? I know Strom left out sometimes when his mama and daddy had gone up for the night or if his daddy was gone out of town — even before Miss Letha and I had got the kitchen shut down — and I wonder if he went there. I wonder if any other colored girls had a baby by him, but if they did, I never heard about it. Or if they had a light-skin baby after they had been with any of those white boys, they wouldn't have known if it was his or whose it was. But my baby was his. It would not have a father. Not one that would ever claim it. That would never happen then or now. Not in Edgefield. Maybe not up here either.

I'd heard about a woman in Old Buncombe girls could go to if they needed to get rid of a baby. The thought of doing that was scary and yet there was a time I wished I knew where she was or how to go about getting there, how much money it would cost. A girl

Mary knew from school at Bettis Academy had died a few days after going there. She got a fever from the procedure and died. But after I felt my baby move the night of the high school students coming to dinner, I wouldn't have done anything to lose her.

Before the school year in McCormick ended, I could hear Strom telling the family at supper that he had been hired for the next year to teach agriculture in Edgefield, but he would have to go to summer school at Clemson for training. Mr. Will agreed with that plan, but there was tension in the room that evening. Letha and I kept quiet in the kitchen waiting for them to ask for coffee, but the only conversation was one or two words between Mr. Will and Strom. Letha sent me in to take the coffee, and I saw Miss Eleanor's eyes were swollen and red. No one wanted coffee. Mr. Will pushed his chair back and stood up.

"Come outside with me, boy."

I could hear them through the raised window in the kitchen — mostly Mr. Will. He hissed at Strom. It sounded like he was talking through his teeth. "You will NOT...." and "I WILL NOT HAVE YOU...," and once it sounded like he said, "That gal in there...." I hear Mr. Strom say, "Daddy, why are you so sure it's mine?" I heard Miss Eleanor's chair scrape the floor and then her footsteps fading up the stairs. When I cleared the table, I saw all their plates nearly full of cold food. My heart was clenched in my throat but still I thought, "At least there's going to be food for me to take home."

I knew Mr. Strom would be leaving soon and wondered if he would say anything to me before he left. The morning he left he came in the kitchen and asked Letha to scramble more eggs than usual. He was wearing a brown suit looked like gabardine, the kind of cloth Aunt Lucy used to make a man's suit. A new suit for his new classes at Clemson. Letha was occupied with the eggs, and I looked over toward Strom. I was thinking he might look at me — I don't know what I expected, but he knew I was going to have a baby — but all he said to me was "Carrie, I need you to fix a sack of food I can take with me on the road." He smoothed his hair back and tightened his tie, stuck his hands in his pockets, moved around the kitchen like he was looking for something, but he did not look at me.

"Here go your eggs, Mr. Strom," Letha tells him.

"Thank you, Letha."

He took his plate into the dining room, ate quick, took one more trip back upstairs, then down, the back screen door banged shut, and he was gone.

Chapter Eleven

NOT LONG AFTER STROM LEFT TO GO TO SUMMER SCHOOL AT Clemson, Miss Eleanor walked into the dining room where I was clearing the breakfast table and told me out of the clear blue sky, "Carrie, I want to let you know we won't be needing you anymore. I believe this will cover what you are owed and then some" and placed five five-dollar bills onto the sideboard, fanned out like a hand of cards, me standing there with a dirty plate and silverware in each hand, feeling like I have been hit in the head. No reason, just said they didn't need me anymore, and that was that. She stepped into the hall, then turned like she forgot something and told me, "Before you go, I need you to go out to the orchard and pick a bushel of peaches and just leave them on the back porch. Letha needs to start pickling some of those before they get too soft. And you may take some home with you." If I hadn't been so obedient back then, I would have left and gone right home, but instead I did what she told me. I went outside and walked down through the yard toward the orchard. I got to the shed. I would have to go inside to get a bushel basket. When I open the door, trapped heat pushes me back. Even in the dark inside of the shed, I see the stain on the floor that is my own blood. I bet it's still there to this day.

It was mid-morning but already hot and so humid. I got out to the orchard and set the basket down between the trees. I was dizzy and felt sick. I reached into the limbs and leaves and plucked peaches until the basket was full, then toted the heavy basket back to the house with sweat soaking through my uniform, and my arms and face itching from peach fuzz. I set the peaches on the porch, picked three off the top to take home, walked down through the back yard and onto the dirt road behind the house and headed home. I didn't tell Letha goodbye.

That was June and the beginning of a hot summer. It had been six months since my mother had passed and I was six months pregnant, my growing belly so strange and secretive now that the three of us moved around it, never speaking about it directly 'til one afternoon when Mae asked, "What we go' name her?"

"Why you saying *her*?" That was Mattie. "It might be a *him*!" We all laughed and the weird spell that had kept us from acknowledging the baby was broken. I knew time had come for me to write Mary and tell her about the baby.

Without the food Miss Eleanor let me take home, I would have to find other work. Mrs. Hardy, who had helped us so much when Mama was sick, knew of someone who needed help doing laundry, so with Mattie and Mae helping, I took in laundry and got a little bit of money from selling eggs from Mama's chickens. Our chickens were about too old to lay, and I knew we'd end up eating them sooner or later.

Mrs. Hardy started planning for what would happen when time came for the baby to be born. She brought over a sack of baby clothes she'd accumulated from people she worked for along with clean rags and a small blanket. She told me when the baby started to come, I might feel a gush of water break out of me, or I might feel pains work their way across my belly. She said send Mattie to get her, and she'd send Lewis to get her cousin who was a midwife. But other plans for me, plans I didn't know about, were in the works, too.

We were in the yard one morning — I guess it was end of September by then — trying to get a fire lit under the washpot when a black automobile drove up slow and stopped in front of the house. Mae moved behind Mattie and they both looked to me. A small lady got out. I recognized her as one of the Thurmond twin sisters, Miss Martha. The sisters were about my age, maybe a year or two older, but I was far removed from them in every other way. Martha was wearing a shirtwaist dress and stylish shoes, the ones with a spool heel and a strap across the top. I took a few steps toward her. I didn't say a word, I was so stunned, and then she told me, "Good morning, Carrie. How are you? We'd like you to go for a ride with us if you will, please. We'd like to talk to you." I look at Mattie and Mae who are dumbfounded, then follow Martha to their car where she tells me, "Please get inside." Both of us reach for the back door handle at the same time and our hands touch, a shock, I think, for both of us.

"Go ahead, climb in," she tells me, and soon as I'm inside, she shuts my door. I'm trapped. I smell leather mixed with their rose-scented powder. Miss Martha gets back in the front seat and twists around to see me better. The other sister, Miss Mary, wrestles the gear shift to where she wants it and the car jerks forward, heading away from my house. She tells me, "Good morning, Carrie." The two of them comment on the trees on Brooks Street changing color, finishing each other's sentences most of the time. I am saying nothing.

Martha said, "We brought a sack of groceries for you and your family. We've been thinking of coming by for a while but our mother …"

Mary interrupts, "We were very sorry to hear about your mother passing."

Then Martha, "Yes, we're so sorry, Carrie. We hope you've been getting along OK. We've missed you at the house. It takes Letha much longer to get dinner ready without your help and …"

"Sister!" Mary interrupts again, silencing Martha with a glance, "I'm sure Carrie doesn't have all day. Carrie, we realize you're going to need some help soon. So, we've made plans to come back for you in a couple of weeks, let's say two weeks from today. If you'll pack your things and be ready to go, I'll honk the horn when we get here."

"Where will I be going?" I asked her, as if I had no choice but to go.

"We hope you'll trust us to have your best interest in mind and that you'll be ready to leave with us."

There's not a word about the baby or why they're coming back for me. Nothing. Miss Mary turned onto the grounds of the First Baptist Church to turn the car around. I noticed the Willowbrook Cemetery beside the church, full of carved tombstones and sculpted monuments, and I thought about Mama. We headed back toward Brooks Street, everyone silent. Mary pulled up in front of my house, left the car running. I didn't move. I didn't know if I was to get out or what.

"All right, Carrie. We'll be back soon." Mary told me looking straight ahead.

Miss Martha got out and opened the door for me. Big as I was by then, I had a hard time getting out. Martha offered out her hand to help me. Her touch this time was not such a shock. Her hand was warm. Once I was out, she gave me the bag of groceries. "We'll see you soon, Carrie," she said, and the car threw up some gravel and dust as it pulled away.

Back inside, Mae took the bag and unpacked the groceries asking me, "What did they say? What did they want?"

"They want me to go somewhere with them when they come back. It's about the baby." I didn't want her to know, but I was scared.

By first of October, we could close the window in the living room and not be bothered so much with flies or by the smell of the hog pens drifting in. Red, yellow, and brown leaves blew into our yard and onto the porch. Wood smoke from the houses on Brooks Street was always in the air now. Mrs. Hardy got to take old copies of *The Edgefield Advertiser* from one of the houses where she worked, so she brought me a stack that we could put over the windows or stuff into the cracks under the door once it got cold. I hadn't had much of anything to read since I left Aunt Lucy's in Augusta. I wanted to read every word in those papers. First one I pick up, right there is an article about Strom and my heart goes to pounding. It said he had resigned his job teaching agriculture and had left Edgefield to take a job with a real estate company in Florida called the Hollywood Company. Said the company expected to transfer him to Richmond, Virginia, when he finished training. I wondered how the school district felt about him quitting when the school year had just got underway, but I knew his daddy could fix anything that needed fixing for Strom. And he wasn't going to have Strom in Edgefield with a colored baby being born when there were people who might know it was Strom's, and there were some people did know. Letha knew. My kinfolks who live on Brooks Street knew where I worked, and they knew. Nothing like that stays a secret for long in Edgefield.

Two weeks after the sisters' visit, I heard the car horn. I got my coat and the pillowcase by the door packed with my clothes and the things Mrs. Hardy had got together for the baby. Mae and Mattie were not home for me to tell them goodbye. I looked around the room, my eyes settled on Mae's empty wire egg basket that had been our mother's.

When I got to the car, Miss Martha lifted a sack full of groceries out from the floorboard and handed it toward me. "We brought a few more things y'all might can use." I dropped my pillowcase down by the car. I looked in the sack and back up at Martha, and told her, "Thank you. My sisters will be awful glad." I took the groceries inside, feeling relief that Mattie and Mae would have food at least for a while. Martha stood waiting for me to get back in the car. There was the smell of the leather and the sisters' powder, the dark cloth lining the inside of the car all around my head, the small glass window from where I saw Martha closing the car door behind me. But I had climbed in just like I had done so many other things people had told me to do, and I shut my eyes as Mary shifted the gears and we pulled away.

I had no idea where they were taking me. I had trusted that they really did have my best interest at heart. Something about

Miss Martha, something kind, made me trust that they wouldn't do anything to harm me or my baby. But once I was in the car, I panicked. Why had I agreed to go? What if they're taking me to get rid of my baby. Can they? Were they going to make me give it up? Could they do that? Or worse? I was scared and there was no one on earth who could help me. I couldn't breathe. Mrs. Alexander, why did I climb into that car? Why couldn't I tell them no?

We drove down Brooks Street headed out of Old Buncombe. I saw a couple of our neighbors peering out to see who was taking me away. Couldn't any of them help me though. We drove out of town and got out on the highway and picked up a little speed and were on our way somewhere — they knew where, but I did not. I have always been able to orient myself, even in the dark, but that day I couldn't get a feel for where we were headed. It wasn't long, maybe less than an hour, when I saw signs saying we were on Highway 25 headed toward the town of Aiken — that's down in South Carolina, too. Half an hour or so and we took a turn down another highway. I sat on my hands waiting to see where they were taking me and what would happen there.

Soon we were in a place called Graniteville. We drove past two churches and a school, all built out of the blue-colored granite stones. On a little farther, we drove through a village of pretty, white houses built along the ridge of a hill. You could see lights through the windows, made me think about Edgefield where some of the houses in town had electric lights by then. When we came to a street with small houses built close together, Miss Mary told Miss Martha, "This must be the Graniteville Textile Mill village." Suddenly the paved road ended and the car bumped onto a dirt road. A ways down that road, we stopped in front of a small, gray house, and a colored lady came out onto the porch. She must've been watching for us. Miss Martha got out and opened the back door for me, reached for my hand, telling me, "Here we are, Carrie."

Mary spoke from inside the car. "Good afternoon, Louvenia. This is the girl I told you about. Carrie, this is Louvenia. She's going to help you with your baby. You'll stay here until we come back for you." It was jarring to hear her say the word *baby*.

Louvenia worked her way down the steps and, looking at me, told them, "I'll take good care of her." Mary thanked her, and the black car took them away. Louvenia picked up the pillowcase, took my elbow to get back up the steps to the screen door, and told me, "Come on inside, baby," where, once again, I did what I was told.

The walls in the front room were papered in a faded flowery pattern. A couch and a pair of chairs covered in a rose-colored velvet took up most of the room. Starched, ruffled curtains framed the front window. Up against the wall was a bed made up neat with a pink bedspread. Off that room I could see the kitchen. Toward the back was another small room. That was where Louvenia took me.

She told me, "Let's leave your things in here and get you a little something to eat." Louvenia shuffled into her kitchen and pulled out a chair for me at the table. Everywhere I looked were jars of powders and dried leaves, other stuff I couldn't tell what it was. Lined up on the windowsill were sprigs of plants she was rooting in glass jars. Louvenia cut open a biscuit and spread a knifeful of molasses on it and poured me some coffee in a tin cup. She sat down across from me, rubbing the hollows between her eyes where her glasses had made little dents.

"So, you are Carrie."

"Yes'm."

"You do some work for Miss Mary?"

"Yes'm. Well, I did work for the whole family. But I don't anymore."

"Does your mama know they brought you here? Where she?"

"My mother passed back in January."

"Oh, I'm sorry, baby. You been gettin' enough to eat?"

"Yes'm, I guess so."

"Are you having any pains yet?"

"No'm, not yet."

Louvenia held out the palms of her hands, small and pale. "God made these small hands strong so I could help babies make their way into this big world, and yours soon gonna be here, too." While I ate the biscuit and coffee, she told me, "Soon as you're done, we'll check to see if we're about ready to have this baby." She rose and pumped water into a pan and washed and dried her hands, then guided me back to the little room and told me to take off my dress and lie down on the bed. I felt embarrassed. I didn't want to undress. Once I worked my dress off my shoulders, she gave me another crisp sheet to cover myself up with. "I know the mattress is hard, but that'll make it easier for you to push down on when the time comes. Now try to relax, Miss Carrie, and let's see where we at." Louvenia helped me lie back, pushed the sheet up from my legs and folded it up over my belly and began to feel for the baby. She pressed the side of my belly with one hand and felt the other side with her other hand. She did the same on the top and bottom of my belly. She said I was lucky the baby's head was down. She took my knees, one in each hand, and spread them apart. I felt myself trying to close them together, but with her elbow she held them still. I stared at the ceiling. I couldn't stop my legs from trembling. She pressed my lower belly with her left hand, then moved the fingers of her right hand up into me very easy and felt all around and thought about it. "We gonna have this baby in a couple days. Here, let's get your dress back on."

"Am I OK? Is the baby gonna be OK? I'm scared I won't know what I'm supposed to do when the time comes."

"Don't you worry. Things will unfold natural. I'm go be right here and everything's gonna be all right. 'Til the time does come, you can help me with the wash I take in if you feel good enough." Louvenia walked me out to the privy back of the house and waited on me until I had finished. When we got to the back stoop, a dirt dauber nest plastered in a corner of the ceiling caught her eye, and she picked up a broom to knock it down. She turned it over, saw it had eggs laid inside, and held onto it. Back in the kitchen I watched her pour about half a cup of what looked like water into a pot — she told me it was gin — then she cut an onion in two and put that in. Last, she crumbled that dirt dauber nest in and cooked it all together on the stove while I sat at the table and watched. Whatever she said or did now, I did not question.

"What will happen when the baby starts to come out? How long will it take?"

"Well now, different folks have different ways to get a baby born. First time sometimes takes a while. Your water might break first, or the pains might come first. Once it starts, we just take things as they come. Do our best to stay calm. I been a midwife granny since I was young as you are now, so don't you worry, baby."

It wasn't but two more days until my time did come. I was out in the yard helping with the laundry. Miss Louvenia had me standing under a chinaberry tree in the shade, throwing wet clothes over tree limbs to dry, when something popped in me, and I felt water running down my legs.

"Miss Louvenia! Something's happened!" I grabbed ahold of the tree out of fear and to keep myself steady. Louvenia had been stirring a washpot full of clothes over a fire. She just tossed her dobbing stick on the ground and kicked some dirt up to the edge of the fire, and without seeming in a hurry, she came and got my arm and walked me into the house and to the bed.

"Ain't nothing to be scared of. Your water done broke, and we will have our baby here before we know it. You be getting your clothes off while I get some water to clean us up a little."

I took off my dress and underwear. Everything was wet. Louvenia came back with a pan of water and some clean cloths and wiped me off, then helped me get into a soft, loose shirt that opened down the front, then helped me lie down. She pulled the sheet up over my shoulders and folded it back straight and even across my chest. She kept telling me, "Don't you worry, everything's gonna be all right, we gonna have a pretty little baby here soon," things like that to keep me calm. While she straightened the sheet under me, she was singing a silly song about going to an animal fair, and that made me smile.

It wasn't long before an awful pain grabbed one side of my belly and crawled over me to the other side. That was the beginning of a long day and night of pains that came like waves, one after the other. Louvenia held my hands and told me to holler if I needed to — not to hold back. The pains came steady all the rest of the morning and all afternoon, and by that evening, time one wave of pain eased, another one rose up. I was so tired by then I would fall asleep between the pains and sleep for a few seconds until another pain would take ahold of me and crawl over my body. Louvenia wiped my face off with a cloth soaked in cool water and wiped my hair back off my forehead.

"Baby, try to breathe in through your nose and out your mouth while you having a pain."

Sometime in the night she bent my knees up and my legs were trembling, and I began to try to push the baby out. She is telling me, "Push. Push hard as you can," and I do push as hard as I can, but the baby doesn't come out. Louvenia takes ahold of the baby's head and pulls and turns it until she can get hold of its shoulders and then I push again *hard*, and I feel the baby slither out into Louvenia's hands. At the same time I feel the baby come out, I feel my body tear apart down there. It burned like fire. She takes the baby and holds it, bent over her hand, and rubs its back real brisk with a towel and soon we hear a tiny cry, sounds like a cat meowing almost, and I know a live baby has been born out of my own body. She lays it up on my chest and tells me, "It's a girl."

Something sank inside me when she said that.

I could see the purple, twisted, ropy cord attached to the baby and running down between my legs and back into my body. Louvenia took a small knife in one hand and held the cord in the other and cut the cord about a hand's length from the baby and tied the end of it to stop the blood. By then the baby was crying, and Louvenia laid her back on my chest. I felt her damp, warm skin against mine. But it wasn't over. She lifted my head so I could drink the potion she made with the dirt dauber's nest to help me push the rest of it out. It tasted horrible, gritty. But soon, what felt like another baby slithered out, and Louvenia quickly scooped it up with all the blood and mess and dropped it all to the floor into a pan and began trying to staunch the blood coming out of me. She pressed wadded up cloths into my open body and kept pressing on me and rubbing my stomach, kneading me like dough and pressing on the rags to stop the blood from coming. I realized I'd been asleep again and now she was quietly gathering up all the bloody cloths and the sheet she had spread under me. She reached up under my back and helped me turn a little to one side so she could move the baby up next to my skin and fold my arms around her. She told me to try to get the baby to nurse to help stop the bleeding. I looked down at this tiny purple thing with soft, damp hair and perfect tiny hands like on a baby doll.

Louvenia held another cup of something warm to my lips for me to drink and told me, "She's a pretty baby. You have to name her something pretty."

"Will you name her?"

"Don't you have someone you want to name her after?

I told her, "My mother was called Getsy, but her real name was Essie, and my sisters are Mary, Mattie and Mae."

Louvenia thought a minute and said, "Let's name her Essie Mae." That was October 12, 1925. Nine months and six days since my mother had died. I was just barely sixteen.

I went through the following days like somebody hypnotized. Louvenia helped me learn to nurse the baby and bathe her. She rocked her and sang to her when she cried during the night. "O, go to sleep, lil baby. O shut your eyes and don't you cry. Go to sleep, lil baby."

Two or three days later I woke up early when the baby cried, and my energy had come back. I ate every bite of everything Louvenia brought me — milk, eggs, pork. My arms didn't tremble when I lifted her out of the cradle Louvenia had put beside my bed. Soon as she cried, my breasts ached, and the milk would let down. Watching Louvenia change her diaper and talk baby talk to Essie Mae, I realized I was hopeful for the first time in a long, long time. Mrs. Alexander, I wish I could thank Louvenia for helping me get through that, but I doubt if she is even still alive. Her name was Mrs. Louvenia Price. That was near Aiken, South Carolina. That baby girl is about grown now.

So, the black car appeared again to take me back home. The sisters sat in the car until Louvenia went out there, and I watched out the window and heard them talk to Louvenia, then tell her, "Have Carrie get her things together and come on out." I saw Miss Mary reach across Martha and hand Louvenia some dollar bills. Louvenia folded the bills and slipped them into her apron pocket.

I felt heartsick all of a sudden. Essie Mae was sleeping. I slipped my hand under her little warm body and her little head like Louvenia had shown me, brought her up to me, and breathed in the baby scent of her neck. Louvenia had to come inside and get me to go on out.

Mary said, "Thank you, Louvenia."

"Yes'm, she did just fine," Louvenia told her, all the while watching me and the baby until we were shut into the car. My tears dropped down on Essie Mae's head. There was a moment we just sat there, nobody saying anything. I waved goodbye to Louvenia and tried to thank her with my eyes. Then Mary got the car turned around and we were headed back toward the highway, back toward Edgefield. Essie Mae began to cry, and I felt my milk let down, so I put her to my breast to nurse her. Martha turned around and looked in wonder, but Miss Mary didn't look at all. She just looked sad at Martha as if she was telling her, "Better not to look back."

Soon we stopped at a filling station and waited in silence while a man pumped the gas. He saw me in the back seat, leaned in close to the small window to where his face was level with mine, then to the sisters he said, "That sure is a pretty little baby you got back here. Which one of you two young ladies is the proud mama?" He thought Essie Mae belonged to one of them. The sisters went stiff. Neither one of them said a word. Mary paid for the gasoline, and we got out of there. I looked down at Essie Mae. Her skin is very light. I didn't want her to look like them, it scared me to think it, but I could see them in her face. I could see the way her top lip goes up in the middle and then curves in a fine line toward the corner of her mouth. Her high forehead. Her eyes, rounder at the corners than mine. She looked like them, especially Martha who is sitting there in front of us. My baby's auntie.

When we got back to Old Buncombe, back home, Mary pulled up and turned off the car engine and sat looking straight ahead. Martha looked down into her lap with her hands folded over the top of her pocketbook, snapping the clasp open and shut, open and shut, with her thumbs. I sat still holding the baby who was sleeping. Mary turned around to face me and told me, "Carrie, we're going to help you as much as we can. We will bring groceries from time to time. And here, we want to give you a little something to tide you over." Then she reached out to me with an envelope, but when I reached to take it, she pulled it back to her chest and told me, "Now we want to make sure you understand some things. You must understand that it's better if you don't talk about any of this. People might get the wrong idea. We're helping you because you were such good help for our family. We don't want anyone thinking there is any other connection because there isn't. Do you understand? As long as you understand, you can expect us to help you." I nodded and she offered the envelope again. I held my hand out and this time she gave it to me.

Miss Martha turned around and said, "We'll see you soon, Carrie. We both wish you good luck, don't we, Mary." She glanced down at my baby again, then turned away. I opened the car door and climbed out, holding the baby in one arm and the envelope and my pillowcase in the other arm, and the sisters looked straight ahead and drove away. They had given me forty dollars that day.

For days on end, Essie Mae cried all the time. One night I was so tired and sleeping so hard I didn't hear her crying until I felt Mae shaking my arm and telling me, "The baby's hungry, Carrie. You got to wake up." Even after I fed her, she cried and cried, her little fists balled up and her lip trembling. I held her above my head and willed my arms to stay still, to keep from shaking her. I did not know what to do to make her stop crying and the night lasted so long. I didn't know it then, but it wouldn't be long 'til I would've given anything if I could've heard her cry one more time.

Chapter Twelve

We made it through that fall and winter with the money the sisters had given me and the help of Mrs. Hardy and some of our other neighbors who brought us food — little bits of cornbread, eggs, greens, a piece or two of fatback. I know it was food they could have used themselves. A tap on our door most mornings would be Mrs. Hardy bringing a cup of milk, one or two eggs, sometimes a piece of pork, maybe some bread. Mattie and Mae usually saved a little bit of their portion for me so I could make more milk for the baby. By dark, we'd all get in Mama's bed, put the baby between me and them, and pull the covers over us and try to keep our body heat in. I had stuck more newspapers into the cracks in our house to keep out the cold, but I remember that being a harsh winter.

Folks helped us in other ways, too. Someone Mrs. Hardy worked for gave her diapers and a few baby clothes her own child had outgrown. Mattie and Mae helped me wash and hang the baby's things all over the house to dry unless it was warm enough outside to hang wash over bushes in the yard without our fingers freezing.

The baby was nursing. Her hungry little mouth latched on to me and sucked hard, but she wasn't filling out, her arms and legs longer but no plumper than when she was first born. I used the rest of the money in the envelope at Christmas and bought food, a rattle toy for the baby, and a coat for Mattie. Mrs. Hardy's son, who had gone North by then, sent her money regularly. By the holidays she had got enough ingredients together to make a fruitcake and brought us half of it. Dried red and green cherries, pineapple, pecans, dates, and coconut baked into a chewy cake. It was the best thing we'd had in a long time. If it hadn't been for her and the other neighbors who helped us and the forty dollars from the sisters, I think we would've starved that winter.

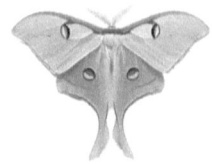

Chapter Thirteen

BY THE NEXT SPRING, WE TURNED A CORNER. AFTER WHAT WE figured was the last frost, Mae planted her garden with seeds she had saved the previous summer. Our chickens started laying more regular, too. Mattie started working two days a week for the lady Mrs. Hardy worked for who usually let her bring home a small service pan. And since the woman was a widow with no children, I didn't have to worry that what happened to me might happen to Mattie. I still got laundry to do, and Mae helped me with it. Every once in a while during that time, the black car would appear and I'd walk out and take the groceries the sisters had brought us. I would carry Essie Mae out on my hip because I was so proud of her, and I believe they really wanted to see her, especially Miss Martha.

Essie Mae hardly cried anymore, and my sisters played with her like she was a baby doll. She was one of us. She slept with me in Mama's bed, and Mattie and Mae moved to a mattress on the floor we'd made and stuffed with feathers and corn husks. Early mornings I would just lie still and watch her sleep, take my finger and touch her fine, curly hair, trace her little eyebrows. I thought about Mama and knew she would have loved Essie Mae if only she could have still been alive. I was beginning to feel older and kind of like I had stepped into the place of my mother. If the baby cried in the night, I would nurse her, and she would go back to sleep. She learned to roll over and sit up and she laughed out loud at Mattie and Mae when they played peek-a-boo with her or sang to her. She could reach for things and had started making happy sounds. She squealed when Mattie or Mae bumped her on their knee and sang Ride that Horsey Down to Town. On days it was warm enough, I'd take Essie Mae out in the yard to get some sunshine. I could just sit and look at her, thinking how beautiful she was, hoping I'd see a resemblance to my mother in her. She was light skinned and it was hard for me to look at her and not see Strom's features — the hazel eyes, straight nose, and curved lips that looked sculpted out of stone. Anyone who knew him would have seen it, too. Those are my memories of her as a baby.

I was sitting on the stoop one afternoon with Essie Mae when the sisters drove up. I carried her to the car. Miss Martha's eyes went right to the baby, eager like she would have loved to hold her, but Mary looked past her toward me.

Martha asked me, "What's the baby's name?"

"Essie Mae, after my mother and sister."

"That's beautiful."

When I turned Essie Mae around so Martha could see her, tears welled up in Martha's eyes when she saw her own family's features there in my baby's face.

Quickly, Mary told Martha, "Sister, please remind Carrie about our understanding and why we want to help out with groceries." Miss Martha said like she had it memorized, "We want to help out because you were a faithful worker at our family's home."

I said, "I understand." Since I was holding the baby, Martha set the groceries on the ground, and I watched them leave. When Mattie unloaded the groceries, she found an envelope in the bag. Inside it was another forty dollars.

I didn't expect to see the sisters again soon, but in a few days, their car pulled up in front of our house and sat there until I went outside. I left Essie Mae inside with Mattie this time. There sat Miss Mary and Miss Martha in the front seat and a man in the back seat who I had never laid eyes on before. Martha told me, "Carrie, this is a family friend we'd like you to meet."

He leaned forward and told me, "Get in the car." I was so stunned that I just stood there until he pushed the door open from inside and I did as he said. Mary shut off the motor. I was in the back seat with this man I did not know. I was terrified, wondering what on earth was happening.

The man told me, "I'll make this clear. There's rumors in Edgefield about this baby that aren't good for the Thurmond family and won't be good for you either. Mr. Strom is coming back to Edgefield and starting a career and one that doesn't need to be derailed by gossip. With this baby in town those rumors will only get worse, especially if you start bringing her out in public. The best thing for you and your baby is for you to send it away." Then he took a thick envelope and told me, "You can use this money to feed yourself and your sisters and help that baby, too, if you do the right thing here. If you don't, there won't be any more help of any kind from the family, and it won't be easy for you to find work here. He told me, "We have sent someone North to your sister and her husband in Pennsylvania who arranged everything for them to take the baby.

I felt stabbed. "You talked to *Mary?*"

He told me, "Have her ready to leave early tomorrow morning. Someone's coming pick her up."

I went crazy. "Miss Mary! Miss Martha! Don't let him do this! I won't ever take her out where folks could see her! Y'all don't have to help me anymore! You don't ever have to come here again! You can't let him do this! Please! Please!"

Miss Mary told me, "Don't be selfish. You must think about what's best for the baby. It's she you should be concerned about."

Miss Martha didn't look back. She didn't say anything. Her head was bowed. The man reached over me, leaned on me, and opened the door for me to get out. I ran next door to Mrs. Hardy who already had the door open for me. I could hardly breathe and when I told her what happened, I was expecting her to tell me how we'd never let them take the baby, how she would help me hide her if we had to. Instead, she told me she was afraid for the baby if it stayed there with us.

"Carrie, I'm afraid the baby might be in danger. Somebody might try to hurt her or worse. Think about who you dealing with and who they connected to. Probably better to let her go with the sisters' man than to risk somebody else taking her. I don't believe the sisters would do anything to put that baby's life in danger. They know she one of them."

"Oh my God. Oh, Mrs. Hardy, no. Oh no! No! No! I can't lose my baby. I can't lose Essie Mae. Oh God no!"

But Mrs. Hardy's warning struck home. I was terrified. I ached to talk to Mary but had no way to do it.

I didn't tell Mattie and Mae. They got into their pallet that night after playing with Essie Mae and were still asleep around five o'clock the next morning when I heard a car pull up, the engine running. I could hardly breathe. Essie Mae was still asleep, so I hadn't nursed her yet or changed her diaper. My breasts were hard and full of milk and aching. I picked her up and wrapped her blanket tight around her and stood still in the dark. Someone knocked light on the door, and I froze, but when he knocked hard, my feet moved me forward, my hand reached out and turned the chunk of wood Daddy had nailed up to lock the door. I realized he was not the same man who had come with the sisters the day before. It was a different car this time, a Tin Lizzy. He told me, "I come for the baby." When he reached out to take my sleeping baby, the backs of his hands touched my breasts as he tried to take her from me. I shudder when I think of that moment.

I pull her back and turn away and whisper, "No! Get out! You're not taking my baby!" Essie Mae begins to scream. Mattie and Mae jump up, terrified, and Mae comes and stands in front of me to shield the baby.

He tells me, "She goes with me and gets to your sister, or she goes with somebody else, and you won't know what happened to her."

I have wondered how I could have turned loose of her. I could have run out the door to Mrs. Hardy. I could have hidden her. But I was afraid of what he had said. Would someone hurt her? Even Mrs. Hardy had been afraid something might happen to her if she stayed with me. It was the most horrible thing I have ever done, but I let him pull her out of my arms. I let go of my baby.

As he was leaving, I told him, "Wait! I have something that has to go with her to my sister," and I got the envelope of money and gave it to him, every bit of the money still in there. What a fool I was to do that. He slipped it inside his coat, then looked past me into the house at Mae and Mattie, turned, and walked to the car where a woman was waiting with the car door open. The man handed Essie Mae to her, her still screaming. The woman took her and slammed the car door, and they were gone. I watched the taillights in the dark, watched my baby going away from me, my warm milk leaking through my nightgown and trickling down my sides, tears running down my cheeks and falling onto my chest. Mae and Mattie are stunned. I fall back in bed and bury my face in the warm place where Essie Mae had just been lying, gasping for breath. I can hear myself wail, a sound like a hurt animal.

Mae shook my shoulders screaming, "Where's he taking Essie Mae? What is going on!"

Once Mattie took in what had happened, she became frantic, screaming "Where's he gone with the baby! O LORD JESUS! WHERE THE BABY?" I fell into Mae's arms. I kept saying, "She's gone! I couldn't help it! I couldn't help it! I can't let anything bad happen to her!" I tried to explain to them why I had to let her go.

Before daylight I lit the lamp and wrote Mary a letter asking her if she had Essie Mae. I walked it to the post office downtown as soon the sun came up.

Unbearable days passed before I heard back from Mary that she did have my baby. I rejoiced and thanked God. I told Mattie, Mae, and myself that if Mary kept Essie Mae just until I saved the money to get us up to Coatesville, she would be safe and have plenty to eat with Mary and John. I swore that before long we would all go up there and be together. Believing that got me through. I would have died if I had known then it would be thirteen years before I would see my daughter again.

I went to work end of that week, but come the week after that, I could not get out of bed. My mind was down in a dark hole and my body felt like it was made of lead. Mattie went to work one or two days a week and on the other days she helped Mae do laundry and weed the vegetable garden. It was Mattie who pulled us through that time. She had two or three families in town now that she did laundry for. She collected it on Mondays. We had a large pot in the yard where she boiled the clothes, scrubbed them on a washboard, then rinsed and starched them and wrung them out. She hung them outside to dry unless it was raining and then brought them inside and hung them up everywhere she could in our tiny house. Once they were dry, Mattie ironed them and then by Saturday she delivered them all back and collected her money. Sometimes if there was even a tiny hole in a shirt or a button was missing, she wouldn't get paid for doing the full load. Sometimes she got paid for a week's worth of laundry when it would be more like three weeks' worth. Most times she got what she was owed. Sometimes she got what she was owed and then some, along with a pan of food.

At night Mattie tried to make me feel better by reading to me from the newspapers Mrs. Hardy brought us and from Mama's Bible. She was getting better all the time at reading, and that soothed my heart, but I couldn't make myself encourage her or ask her to keep on reading. I would just turn toward the wall in Mama's bed and lie there silent. Mae would come and sit on the edge of the bed so I could feel her presence, but I couldn't talk to her either and I got to where I couldn't eat. I felt like I was falling down a hole that didn't have no bottom. Mrs. Hardy began to come over late in the evenings when she got home from her work and read to me like she had read to Mama from the Bible. She read me the story about Paul and Silas when they were jailed in the innermost part of the dungeon, their ankles in chains, but they prayed and had faith, and a mighty earthquake shook the dungeon and the walls fell down and their chains fell off. Mrs. Hardy shared her food with us and told Mattie to open the door in the morning to let in sunlight. Eventually, I got back up and washed myself and started helping Mattie with the laundry and began to feel hungry again.

The first thing I did after I made that turn was to write Mary another letter. I told her all about having the baby with Miss Louvenia in Graniteville and how the sisters had come and how the man had terrified me and why I had no choice but to do what they said. It gave me a hollow feeling to write that because as soon as I put it down on paper, I was already wondering if I couldn't have stood up to the sisters and not given the baby to the man. I still have the agony of wondering that to this day. I told her, "Please write and tell me who came up there to talk to you about taking the baby and how you and John feel about keeping her for me until I can get up there." I asked her to tell me how Essie Mae was doing and whether she was adjusted to the new surroundings. What she could do now. Could she talk? What did she like to eat? I asked her if she could send me a picture. I told her Mae and Mattie were doing pretty well and how much we missed her and the baby both and how much I loved them. I asked her if the man gave her the envelope with the money in it and told her to get Essie Mae a pretty baby dress with some of it and tell her it's from her mama.

The letter I got back from Mary nearly broke my heart. I was happy because she told me how good Essie Mae was doing and that she had cried for a couple of days but then she started smiling and reaching out to her and John. She told me Essie Mae was growing like a weed and could say "Mama" and "Dada." That right there sent a pain through my heart because it meant Mary was thinking of herself, not me, as Essie Mae's mother. I thought how dare she do that. She said she was sewing clothes for Essie Mae and making sure to take her out to get fresh air and sun every day and that one of her neighbors who had also gone up there from Old Buncombe had a baby girl the same age as Essie Mae and she and that baby's mother were letting them play together and teaching them to share. She said she was telling Essie Mae stories and reading to her from a little book of rhymes and singing to her every day. John was working at the steel mill and getting paid every week and they had plenty to eat and a small but nice house to live in. Mary and John had a nephew, Calvin, living there, and Mary said first thing Calvin did whenever he came in the house was to pick up Essie Mae and play with her. They all loved her, I could tell. And she sent me a picture of Essie Mae. I still have it in my things at Mary's. She's sitting in a little wicker basket with a lacy dress on. It's in one of those thick paper frames with an oval cut out where her picture is. Her pretty face is looking straight at the camera. Her lips are parted just a little, like a rose bud about to open. Soft little curls frame her round face, and light coming from behind makes her look like a baby angel.

It was clear Mary was happy to have Essie Mae and that Essie Mae was in a good place and was being well taken care of. I was thankful for that, but I was so sad that I was not part of her life. But the truth is, I know if Essie Mae had stayed with me in Edgefield, she might have been in danger. Also, she would not have had all those things Mary was giving her. And even if folks here left her alone, she would've had a hard time in Edgefield with her light skin and the rumors that would've swirled around her. I wished I had been able to do for her what Mary was doing. I wish I could have run away with her when she was a baby, but I wasn't able to do that. You understand, Mrs. Alexander? I loved her but I let her get away from me.

Oh, and the man who took her — he did not give Mary the envelope of money. I was foolish to have trusted him. He stole that money, and he was probably paid to take my baby away to begin with.

I was headed to the dark place again, but I told myself that by Christmas I would have saved enough money to take Mattie and Mae and go north to Coatesville. We would have Christmas presents for Essie Mae and Mary, fruitcake, and warm coats to wear up there. I would make and save enough money by then.

The doctor who admitted me here in the hospital made rounds today. He came over and called me Mrs. Clark and asked me if I needed anything. He remembers everybody's name. I can see it hurts him to see us suffer. He told me he would get the nurse to up my dose of pain medicine and I will surely appreciate that. I asked him how long I've got but he said nobody knows when their time will come.

Chapter Fourteen

By early summer 1926, Essie Mae, now eight months old, had been gone two months. I had the picture of her that Mary had sent and one of the gowns that still held her baby scent. Believing we would all get to Pennsylvania within the year energized me and motivated me to get back to work. Mattie had a few days a week working as a maid. Mae's garden was helping feed us, and all of us were doing laundry. I got work two days a week in another house on Penn Street doing the same kind of work I'd done at the Thurmonds'. I was treated fair there and, although the people I worked for sometimes paid me in food or clothes instead of money, the food was good, and the clothes were in better shape than ours.

The three of us started back going to church meetings when we could walk there or get a ride with a neighbor who had room for us in their wagon. One Sunday, Reverend Vaughn told us he was organizing a fundraiser to help out Bettis Academy. This was the school Mary and I had been to way back. It was started by

Reverend Alexander Bettis who had been a slave in Edgefield. The wife of the man who had owned Mr. Bettis had taught him to read, but he never did learn to write. After he was freed, he became a Baptist preacher and started a lot of churches down around Edgefield and then he started a school. Reverend Bettis is to thank for so many people learning to read and write and getting an education — you can't imagine what all he did. Bettis Academy taught the Bible and reading and writing, and home economics and agriculture, too.

Back at the beginning of the school, every July Fourth Reverend Bettis held a celebration out on the school grounds. Starting at the early light of dawn, drill teams with wooden rifles marched and chanted 'til the marching turned into dancing and the chanting turned into singing. That celebration was going on even back when I was a child. There was food and ice cream. It's one of the few celebrations I can remember where so many colored folks got together, and their spirits were happy.

But ever since Bettis Academy was built back then, it was always in need of funding and Reverend Vaughn, the new preacher at Macedonia Baptist Church, organized fundraisers to help out. Mattie and I decided to go to the next fundraiser which was going to be a dance. Mattie was especially committed because she was determined to get as much education as she could. Mae still struggled to read with my help, but she kept trying. She didn't want to go to a dance, but she was happy about me and Mattie going.

That evening, Mattie and I tried on all the dresses we had to see what we could wear to the dance. We were actually giggling thinking about going to a dance — something we had never done.

Mattie tried on a dress Mama had worn but she couldn't button it. Neither one of us was as small and thin as Mama had been. I pulled a dress over my head that Aunt Lucy had made me years ago. It slipped over my head and shoulders, but it was faded and threadbare and too short. But when we looked at each other, we got to laughing real hard at how we looked. Mae laughed, too. It was one of those times when you forget everything and just laugh. All of us felt happy that night.

Around that time, though, I got a jolt one afternoon when I read in a paper Mrs. Hardy brought us that Strom had come back to Edgefield and that he was teaching and coaching at Edgefield High School. It sounded like he was doing all kinds of things that would get him noticed and help build up his reputation. He had started an organization called the Baptist Young People's Union and started a summer camp for farm boys and he had been appointed to the Edgefield School Board. He was even working with Mrs. Modjeska Simkins to get dental work for children in the colored schools. You've heard of her work to help the colored in South Carolina? I started shivering at the thought of him being back in Edgefield.

It wasn't any time — about two or three days — before a car pulled up at our house one rainy morning and when I looked out, I saw it was the Thurmond sisters, so I pulled my coat over my head and went out. They left the car running with the windshield wiper slapping back and forth. Miss Martha put down the window and Mary leaned toward me and said, "Carrie, our father asked us to bring you this envelope. He asked us to let you know it was from him and to tell you that he hopes you are getting along well. She reached over Martha and handed me the envelope and they drove away. Why had Mr. Will told the sisters to tell me the money was from him? His name had never come up before when the sisters had brought me money or groceries. I looked into the envelope and saw a fat coil of bills. It was later that night before I could touch it and put it into my savings jar.

Odd as it seems, some of that money led to an event that would end up changing my life. I decided that on our next trip to get groceries, we would use a little of that money to buy cloth to make dresses to wear to the dance. Have you ever been in the South, Mrs. Alexander? Stores there are different from stores up here. At least the general store in Edgefield is. It sells about everything you need, from groceries, to tools, to cloth. So, on our next trip into town, after we got our groceries, we went straight to where the bolts of cloth were wedged side by side on a shelf toward the back. Some of that cloth had been there so long, the curve of the fold was dusty and faded. We looked through the bolts until we made our choice of a silk broadcloth. Mattie liked a powder blue color, and I picked out a mint green, then we selected thread that matched the cloth. What caught our eye most though was a dress pattern on display next to the cloth that said on the front "McCall's Goes to Paris to Bring Paris to You." The sketch showed a woman in a stylish dress like we had never seen before. I held the pattern up close to study it while Mattie stood on her tiptoes and looked over my shoulder. The dress bodice was straight and long. It came down below the waist with buttons down the front, it had a long sash tie collar, and long sleeves with a cuff at the wrist. The skirt was pleated and a lot shorter than all the dresses we had ever seen — looked like at least eight or ten inches above the ankle. The pattern showed three different views, so we could make ours be a little different from each other. We told the clerk which cloth we wanted cut and handed him the pattern. The whole time I could feel him looking at me. He pulled the bolts out and plopped them on the counter and measured out what we asked for. Before he cut it, he took a pencil stuck over top of his ear and a tablet and figured how much we would owe, then asked, 'You gals got enough money to pay for this cloth?" We told him, "Yes, sir." So, he cut and wrapped our cloth, the spools of thread, and the pattern, and we paid and started home, going on about how stylish our new dresses would be. We would be beautiful. I remember thinking Edgefield smelled good, like honeysuckle and confederate jasmine. One thing that's different up here in Philadelphia, if you're walking downtown and you meet a white person coming toward you, you just keep walking. In Edgefield, you step out of the way for white folks. On the way home that afternoon, Mattie and I stepped aside several times to let folks pass, and every time, I felt them turn around and look at us. Were they gossiping about me? I walked home wondering if most people in Edgefield knew about my baby or was I just imagining they did. Soon the heat of the afternoon air and the humidity brought out the smell of the hog pens again.

I would have to sew at every spare minute to finish our dresses in time for the dance. When we got home, Mae had swept the floor so we could spread out our cloth. Between the two of us and with Mae helping, we got them cut out before we went to bed that night. While Mattie and I worked, Mae sewed some of the seams I had carefully pinned, and I would sew at night. A few days before the dance, our beautiful dresses were finished. I wished my Aunt Lucy, the one taught me how to sew in the first place, could have seen them. I watched as Mattie tried hers on and then I put mine on. I thought the colors were perfect on us. Her blue and my mint green made us look fresh and alive. We looked at each other and were so happy that we held hands and danced around the floor with Mae laughing. Mae soaked up other people's feelings, happy or sad.

The day of the dance Mattie and I worked. Mae baked cookies for us to take to get in to the dance. When I got home, Mae had plaited Mattie's hair and helped her get into her dress. Mae brought me some water and a rag to wash off from the day's work before I put my dress on. Then she brushed and plaited my hair the same as Mattie's and stood back smiling like our mother used to, happy at how beautiful we looked. It was still light when we left out walking to the church. Although I was anxious, I was still excited about this new experience we were about to have. But the dance turned out to be like a lot of things, the looking forward to it and getting ready had been more fun than the dance itself.

When we went in, we laid our cookies on a table with the other baked donations where Reverend Vaughn's wife sat. She would take them the next day to the Ladies' Mission bake sale. A windup record player set up on the table beside her sent music out into the room. The song playing when we got in, I still remember, was "Lost Your Head Blues." A few kerosene lanterns made a soft glow around the room. Wildflowers in bottles sat on the window ledges and sheets hung against the walls gave a clean, soft look to everything. Tables and chairs had been moved out of the center of the room to make a space for dancing.

As proud as I was of our dresses, seeing the other girls in old dresses and dresses that no longer fit made me feel uncomfortable, guilty. I tried to focus on the music and watch kids having fun dancing, not to think too hard about anything. A girl we knew named Madora we hadn't seen in a long time rushed over and hugged us. "Y'all look beautiful. It's so good to see you. How is Mae?" When a few boys started to gather around us, Mattie's face lit up. Me, though, I was uneasy with the attention. Then I saw a cousin of ours everybody called Coot walking over, focusing on me and smiling, her chin raised a little and her eyes half closed. When we were little one time at church, the Sunday School teacher asked Mae to read something out of the Bible. Mae stared at the tissue-thin page of her Bible for what seemed like forever 'til Coot realized Mae couldn't read. "Is Mae a re-tard?" Coot asked, and the other children giggled. Mae was humiliated. I never did like Coot after that. So she walked over to us at the dance and asked me, loud enough for everybody around us to hear, "Hey, Tunch, how is your baby doing?" I was as caught off guard as if she had thrown a pan of cold water on me. The excitement I had been feeling about the dance and the music and my new dress evaporated. Mattie took my hand and held it. I was speechless, but then a guy I didn't know stepped in front of Coot and asked me to dance. I went to him, anything to keep from answering Coot's question.

It was Willie Clark. He was dressed in a real suit with a vest. He took my hand and pulled me toward him and put his hand around my waist. He complimented me on my dress, said it was very stylish, and turned me around to get a good look at it, nodding his head up and down and smiling. That got me right there. While we danced, he began the conversation asking me if I knew much about Bettis Academy. He was impressed when I told him I had gone to school there as well as in Augusta. Considering the anxiety I felt after Coot's question, I was surprised by how easy our conversation flowed.

Willie told me, "They need a teacher at the colored school in Edgefield. You ought to try to get a job teaching."

"Me a teacher?" The thought of it was flattering.

"Why not? Tell me what you studied when you were in Augusta."

So I told him about Velma and school, and while we were dancing, Mrs. Vaughn put a slow song on the record player. Willie tightened his hold at my back and pulled me closer to him. I felt my palms getting sweaty but tried to dance gracefully, but when he tightened his arm around me, pulling me even closer, the panic I had the first time Strom did that to me in the hall upstairs came back from somewhere deep in my brain. I stiffened and thanked him but pulled away and wove through the other dancers back to where Mattie was standing. As I stood there in the noise of the music and the people talking loud and laughing, I whispered to Mattie, "We have to go."

Mattie had been talking with a boy we knew from church and was enjoying the dance. "You can leave if you want to, but I'm staying!" Still, I pulled her away, and, not wanting to make a spectacle of us, she followed me, and we ducked out of there as quiet as we could. Mattie was angry at me and didn't say a word to me the rest of the night.

As we walked home, I felt ashamed. I thought about the money I had used to buy our cloth and wished instead that I had added it to my savings to go North. But making those dresses to go to the dance changed my life. For one thing, word got around about the dresses I had made myself and Mattie and not long after, Mrs. Edna Seabury, the wife of the preacher at the First Baptist Church, came to our house on Brooks Street to ask if I would make her daughter's wedding dress. As her eyes wandered around our small living room, she told me she had heard about the dresses from her maid who'd said how stylish they were. Hadn't anybody in Edgefield ever complimented me on something I had done, and I was so proud. She described the wedding dress her daughter wanted made and I told her I would do the best I could.

The next week she brought me yards of candlelight silk and lace, little buttons that had to be covered in fabric, stays to sew into the bodice, and a Vogue wedding dress pattern. She had gone to Atlanta to buy the silk and the lace. Her daughter came along for me to take her measurements and as soon as they left, I got to work cutting out the thin paper pattern pieces. While I did that, Mae cleaned the floor so I could lay the cloth down on it and cut the pieces out. I'd never worked with fabric that expensive, and I had to be extremely careful. I could not make a mistake.

I sewed for several weeks and when I had almost finished it, Mrs. Seabury brought her daughter over to try it on. Mae put the blanket we used to divide our room down on the floor so the dress tail wouldn't get dirty and when the daughter got the gown on and looked down at how beautiful it was, she squeezed my hands and tried to dance me around the room. We all laughed and in that small dim house that afternoon, the same place where my mama had died, I was happy for that young girl, for her mother, and for myself.

I sewed every minute I could -- early in the morning and late at night by the kerosene lamp and wore my fingers out with the needle and thread stitching that beautiful silk dress. In a few weeks, it was done and Mrs. Seabury came to pick it up. The daughter tried it on again and her mother got tears in her eyes at how beautiful she was in that white wedding gown. She pressed my hand and thanked me, then she paid me what we had agreed on plus five extra dollars. I felt a great sense of accomplishment that day.

At the daughter's wedding, word got around about who had made her dress, and after that, I almost always had a dress to make someone in Edgefield — other rich, white women like Mrs. Seabury but some for colored folks, too. I would go by the pattern they brought me, but I would add something of my own to make it unique. The money I made ranged from whatever somebody could pay for colored, to whatever I charged for white, and my savings to go North grew slow but surely.

Besides getting work sewing for people, another thing that came from my night at that dance was I started to talk to Willie Clark. He came to our house one evening and introduced himself, asked if we remembered him from the dance at church. We sat out in the yard 'til dark — me, Mae, Mattie, and Willie. After that night, Willie showed up a couple of times a week. He was always dressed in a clean shirt and pressed pants, but the clothes I had on and had been wearing all day at work sometimes embarrassed me. When Mattie complimented him on his clothes, he said his mother told him that wearing nice clothes was one way for people to express who they were. She might not have had but one Sunday dress, he said, but she had made herself a pretty one and did the same for him and his brothers and his sister. He told funny stories about his brothers and sister, and you could tell a strong bond held them together. His mama and daddy were clearly the most important people in his life. He started coming to the house often, and it was soon clear that it was me he was coming to see.

Before long, I went for walks with Willie. We walked from our house on Brooks Street to town and back, talking the whole time, usually getting back to my house right about dark. At first, we talked about school and what all I learned about in Augusta, like we had done at the dance. Then one evening when we got to town, Willie pointed out Mr. Strom's law office. I was taken by surprise, though, when he mentioned my baby. He already knew about her and who her daddy was.

"How did you know about that, Willie?"

He told me, "There's a lot of people know it. Does he ever help you out any?"

"His sisters did at first, but now my baby lives up North. As soon as I save enough money, I'm moving to Pennsylvania, where she is with my sister."

"Why don't you do something to get him to help you, give you the money to go to her?"

What did he think I could do? Our talk ended after that, and we walked home without saying anything else.

Willie's daddy was Jerry Clark. He owned a beautiful piece of land he farmed, and Willie worked on it together with his brothers and his sister. His mother, Genie, and his daddy both could read and write and had taught all their children to. Willie had been raised different from most of the people I knew. His family owned a radio and could get news about things going on in the world. With his two brothers, he had joined the NAACP — I hadn't ever heard of it back then. He explained to Mattie and me what it stood for and why all colored people should join it.

"Y'all might not be aware of the danger we all in."

"What kind of danger?"

"It's mostly men and boys that's got to watch out, but anybody can be a victim. Take Carrie there, for instance. She's been a victim. But no white man is gonna get in trouble for doing something to a colored woman."

Mattie and Mae looked to me to see how I would react to that. None of us knew what to say. We were all uncomfortable, but Willie was one to say whatever he thought.

"A lot of white men consider it a rite of passage to have relations with a colored girl." He told us a white man drove up to him in front of the courthouse downtown last summer and asked out the window, "Boy do you know where I can get me a nigger girl for a few hours?" Again, we were embarrassed to silence.

Willie was the first person I ever heard talk about Jim Crow. I asked, "Who is Jim Crow?" That unleashed all kinds of revelations that I had not ever realized or thought about. Same things that burned Willie up inside. He told me, "Down here in the South, whites can do whatever they want, to whoever they want. Colored boys might be arrested for some made-up crime and hauled off to jail and made to work off a fine they never owed in the first place just so somebody could get free work out of them. Those boys are no better off than slaves. Laws all over the South keep colored people as bad off as when they were slaves."

Since his daddy owned his own land and didn't have to give most of what he raised to a landlord, their family wasn't as poor as most other people I knew. Willie brought us produce from his daddy's farm — tomatoes, potatoes, beets, corn. It was the first time in a long time that we had enough to eat. He had money from time to time and bought all of us treats like chocolate or snuff. We had never dipped snuff, so Willie showed us how to put it between our cheek and gum or behind our lower lip. All of us got to laughing and spitting it out except Mae. She liked it and used it every time Willie brought her some.

The more I was with Willie, the more I wanted to be with him. I got to where I could let him kiss me when we'd get back from our walks without freezing up. I even liked it when he rubbed my arms and put his hands on me, as long as he was slow and talked me through it. I'll never forget one evening when we got back to my house and he held my face in his hands and told me, "Carrie, you are beautiful." That really stole my heart.

But Willie couldn't be with me without bringing up Strom Thurmond. He said I had to *do* something about it. He said, "Just think what would've happened to any Black man around here if he had done the same to one of Strom's sisters! He'd been swinging from a tree with his dick cut off!" But what he thought I could do, I do not know. If you are colored in the South, you might as well get used to the way things are. A colored cannot hold a white person accountable for anything. Not in a court. Not anywhere. There was no way I could have tried to take on my baby's daddy. That plus being hungry most of the time were both reasons why I couldn't think about doing anything that involved Strom. I came to suspect that Willie's interest in me probably began with his resentment toward Strom Thurmond.

We did get along all right, we got more familiar with each other, and it was good -- for a while. I was expecting that he might ask me to marry him. But the good times we had always came to an end when his thoughts turned to how there was no fairness for colored. We would be having a good time, maybe a romantic date, but before the night was over, he would start to harp on the things that tortured him, and there was no end to the things that tortured Willie.

Willie knew a man named Jim McKie who was lynched in Edgefield along with his father and brother-in-law. The father was a successful farmer like Willie's daddy. He was running in an election to be postmaster. Folks didn't want him to get that job took their anger out on his son. The son was shot so many times they had to shovel up his body in pieces. Two years later Jim McKie's wife tried to get a settlement from the government. Willie said it was Strom's own daddy, Mr. Will, who spoke out against her and said those darkies deserved what they got because of their own conduct.

A man Willie's daddy was kin to named Butler Middleton was shot by a white mob. A bunch of colored men got accused of shooting a gun near a white man's house and a mob of white men came after them with guns and ropes. The colored men hid inside a house, but the white men fired bullets into the house and one hit and killed Butler Middleton. Nobody was arrested.

Another man Willie heard of who they said stole a Bible and some furniture from a church was beat to death by a white mob. Then they beat his mother to death for trying to save him.

Willie knew of a boy up toward Greenville, he wasn't but seventeen years old, who was taken from the jail by a mob of men, one of them being a member of the state legislature. They said he had raped an eleven-year-old white girl. They tied a rope around one of his feet and swung him from a telephone pole and shot him full of four hundred bullet holes. They cut off his fingers and passed them out in the crowd for souvenirs. They even cut the rope they hung him with into small pieces and gave out those pieces of rope for souvenirs.

Another man had his head and right arm and his fingers and privates cut off for souvenirs and his body was singed and hung by a noose in the town square. Willie made me look at a *postcard* he had of a Black man hanging from a tree. His body had been burned so bad it looked like a log out of the fire. And on and on.

One boy Willie was most troubled by was a boy from over in Eutawville who was arrested for cursing at a white man who had raped the boy's sister. That boy got drug out of jail, whipped, and his privates cut off, then they weighed his body down with an iron grate and threw it in the Santee River. Willie asked me could I not see the *irony* in that.

I worried about Willie's own life. One minute he'd be talking about somebody getting lynched and how it could happen to anybody if they made a wrong move, and the next minute he'd be talking about colored getting even, rising up, taking their place. To this day, I often think about all those people who were beaten or shot or burned or hanged. Probably some of them been forgotten except maybe by their families, and after their families are gone, won't be anybody ever knew they even lived.

The main difference between Willie and me, I guess, was that after I came back from my aunt's in Augusta, I wasn't in circumstances where I could think past the next day — with Mama sick and me having to go to work and wondering about how we were going to eat. Then me having Essie Mae. Willie had had time to think about things that went way beyond just getting enough to eat and keeping a baby alive.

I was in love with Willie, though. Looking back, I see how attractive he was — not just to me but to everybody. For one thing, he was handsome — straight and tall, slim with a big smile and kind eyes. His skin was dark and rich. He wore his clothes well. Everybody who knew Willie knew how good he was to his mama and daddy and to his brothers and his sister. He was the oldest and his daddy couldn't have run their farm without Willie's help. He was smart, too, from knowing about planting and raising livestock to knowing about things going on in the world. And he made people he liked feel good by the serious way he listened to them when they talked, the way he leaned toward you when you talked like he was hungry for what you had to say. But he hadn't *really* listened to me the times I told him I was going North to be with Essie Mae as soon as I could.

Chapter Fifteen

AFTER WE HAD BEEN COURTING FOR A FEW MONTHS, WILLIE took me to meet his family. They were all so proud of him, especially his mother who didn't take her eyes off him or stop smiling when he talked. It was beautiful to see how comfortable his mother and father were in their lives, but also heartbreaking to think of my own mama and daddy and how much they had struggled. Like he had told me, his mother dressed nice, even just working at home cooking and cleaning. Willie had told her I could sew, and when I told her about the wedding dress I had made, she told me, "You and I might have to make you a wedding dress someday." That embarrassed me a little, but I knew it meant she was accepting me, and that was a good feeling. I liked all his family, and I could tell they liked me. I felt like I belonged there. Meals we had at their house were a lot of fun, all of us around a big farm table with food they had grown themselves, with no talk of the horrible things that preoccupied Willie when it was just him and me together.

The night Willie asked me to marry him, he showed up at our house after dark when I wasn't expecting him. He usually came end of the week and this was early in the week. I had come home from work dirty with a pan of food for us, and Mattie was dividing it out on our plates. Willie sat down and told me, "Go ahead and eat. Take your time." But with him waiting there, I couldn't eat and told Mae and Mattie to go on and not wait on me. Out on the porch Willie pulled a newspaper from under his coat and held a folded section up in my face. I told him, "Willie, what you doing? I can't even see out here. It's too dark!"

He shook the paper at me. "Look here at this. Mr. Strom done passed the bar and going into practice with his daddy here in Edgefield. He didn't even go to law school, Carrie! How does somebody pass the lawyer exam and they ain't ever gone to law school! Must be nice to just glide through doors like he does! Hell, I think I'll just go be a goddamn lawyer my own self!"

I pulled away. "Why you showing me that? I don't know what you think that means to me! I wish you wouldn't tell me anything about him! Can't you forget about him?"

"Sorry, I thought you might want to know what your baby's daddy was up to! How he's a lawyer now and didn't even go to law school!"

"He went to court and watched his daddy being a lawyer! He studied his daddy's books. You don't know what he did! You don't know everything!"

"So now you taking up for him? Goddamn, Carrie, you not right!"

I turned so fast and went back inside and slammed the door. Mae and Mattie, still at the table, stared at me with a look like

"What was that all about?" Mae told me, "Carrie, you better come finish your supper."

I sat back down and took a few bites, but it was like I was eating straw. Mattie cleaned up the table and they got in bed, and I did, too. I lay there awake, rattled, thinking about all what Willie had said. I couldn't sleep. Then sometime into the night I dozed off when a light knocking on the door woke me up and scared me. Mae woke up frightened, too, and stared at the door while I went to see who was there. Willie called from outside, "Carrie, can you come out here a minute? I need to see you. Just for a minute. OK?" I told Mae to go on back to sleep and I went out in a raggedy shirt belonged to Daddy and my hair tied in a rag. Willie reached out and took me in his arms and held me and told me he was sorry. He told me, "Look. I been thinking hard about things. I don't know why I let things get to me like they do. From this day on, I'm telling you, I won't throw that stuff in your face anymore. Carrie, you mean more to me than anything else in my life. I love you. I think you are brave and beautiful, and I want to marry you."

I had gone from standing there angry and stiff to taking a deep breath and softening a little. "You know I'm going to Pennsylvania soon as I can?"

He kissed me on the cheek and told me, "We can work it out. You think about it. I got to get back before Mama gets worried. She'll think I've done got picked up."

He held my hand as he backed away until our fingertips slipped apart.

The rest of that night I stayed awake, excited, wondering how we would work things out. I thought that with the money I could make sewing for people and the money he made farming with his daddy, we could save enough to go to Pennsylvania and take Mae and Mattie with us up to Mary's. We could get my baby and raise her as a family. Essie Mae was five years old by then and plenty young enough to learn to love Willie and think of him as her father. Maybe Mary's husband could get Willie a job at the steel mill, I could sew for people, and surely Mattie and Mae could get work cleaning or doing laundry up there. If we could get a place close to Mary and John, Mary could be like a second mother to Essie Mae. And maybe up there Willie could forget about Jim Crow and all the other things that stirred inside him.

I was so hopeful. I should have known better than to think all those possibilities would work out. Mainly, Willie was not cut out to work in a steel mill. He worked the farm like his daddy did and their land meant something to him that I didn't understand. Also, down deep I wondered could Willie ever learn to love Essie Mae with her real father being a man he despised.

I couldn't let go of this dream. Before many more weeks passed, there I am walking to the church with Willie to get married. It was early fall and Edgefield was crisp and smelled of folks burning woodfires. I am wearing the dress I made myself when me and Mattie went to the dance where I first met Willie. Willie is all dressed up in a dark brown double-breasted suit with a thin tan stripe in it. A little square of yellow cloth is sticking up out of the breast pocket of his suit. He has on two-tone, brown and white shoes and a pair of yellow leather gloves that match the pocket square. I had never seen a man wear fancy gloves and my stomach tightened a little. He was very handsome, but I bet the cost of those gloves and shoes could have fed my family for a week.

Willie held my hand as we walked to Mt. Canaan Church where the new preacher, Reverend Taylor, would marry us after the church service. Genie walked beside me with her arm through mine, and Jerry, Willie's daddy, walked beside him. Mae and Mattie followed behind us with Willie's brothers and his sweet sister who adored Willie as much as his mother did. Mattie carried Mama's bible for me to hold while I said my vows and Mae picked little vines with shiny green leaves along the way until she had a fistful to hand me for a bouquet. I wish Mae was here now, Mrs. Alexander. Mattie, too. I wish they were both here with me now.

Walking up to the preacher, I felt like I was going to be sick. Sweat trickled down my sides underneath my dress. I was seventeen years old. Willie was twenty-five. I didn't know for sure why I was marrying Willie Clark except sometimes I felt in love with him. I knew I'd be safe and have somebody to feel joined to and not be alone. I knew I'd be with a family who loved each other like my own family had. I thought we would have enough money not to ever be hungry. I thought he would go with me to Pennsylvania to be with Essie Mae.

When preaching was over, we walked to the front of the church, Willie smiling and leading the way down the aisle to where Reverend Taylor was standing looking toward us. Reverend took my hand and placed it in Willie's hand and started the ceremony.

"Dearly beloved, we are gathered here to join this man and this woman in holy matrimony." I looked over at Mae whose eyes were shut tight, her head was bowed down and her bottom lip was quivering. Sunlight coming in the window made shadows under her features and Mae was beautiful at that moment. Mattie was standing up tall looking straight at me and Willie, smiling with tears brimming up in her eyes. We repeated our vows, then it was over with, and I was married to Willie Clark. Willie slipped a gold band, thin as a piece of wire, onto my finger. Reverend Taylor ended with "Till death do you part."

Our first night together as man and wife was a little awkward for everyone. His mama had fixed a big supper, so I made myself eat not to hurt her feelings. We sat at the table making conversation until his mama got up to clear the table and I got up to help her, but she said, "No bride should be washing dishes on her wedding night. You get on out of here!" That took a little of the strain off and everybody laughed, and Willie got my hand and we said goodnight and went to our room. It was a small room built off the back of the house. I squeezed over into the corner to undress. Willie took his clothes off and laid them on a chair. I laid my dress on top of his clothes, and we got in the bed. As bad as I wanted to feel happy, I couldn't stop shaking. Willie pulled me up close to him and told me how lucky he was to have me for his wife. He took my hands and teased me about how cold my hands always were. He always would say, "Cold hands, warm heart." When we started to make love, I smelled that scent on me that had never left my memory since I was out in that shed, and I worried that Willie could smell it, too. Willie held me after it was over until he fell asleep and I would lay there awake for a while. I had stopped bleeding after Essie Mae was born and while I still had her and was nursing her, and I never had started back to bleeding so I thought I would not be able to have another baby.

Every day was pretty much the same. Willie came in from work about dark most days and I did, too, on days I worked as a maid. I cooked at one of my two jobs, so I had to stay until after the family had finished eating and get the kitchen cleaned and closed down. On days I was home, I sewed 'til time to help Genie cook supper, then we ate when all of us were home. Willie was always ready for me and him to go to bed after supper, and once we were in bed alone, he always told me he loved me. I remember wishing I could give 100 percent of myself to him and our marriage, but I never did. I always felt the pull of my lost daughter.

Around this same time, Mrs. Hardy's son, Lewis, came down for a visit. He had gone North to Chicago and got work in a meat-packing plant. I had gone home to check on Mattie and Mae one afternoon when Mrs. Hardy brought Lewis over to say hello to us. Right off the bat, I could see Mattie was sizing him up and he was her, too. In the years since they had seen each other, they had both grown up. The few days he was home, he walked over to talk to Mattie. She had become a good reader by then, and Lewis told her about books he had read and about a whole group of colored writers and artists and singers up North. Lewis told Mattie about ideas blooming up North and the freedom colored people had up there. He said some whites up there didn't want to work with coloreds, didn't want to use the same bathrooms or have the same jobs, but still colored people had it better there than they did here. When Lewis left, he told Mattie he would write. No sooner had he been gone for a few days when a letter came from Lewis. He had copied some poems down and mailed them to Mattie and she read them out loud to me and Mae. One of them about someone whose daddy was white and his mama was Black made tears come to my eyes. The person in the poem was sad, didn't know if he was white or Black. Mattie wrote him back. She wanted me to read over the letter to check it for spelling, but after handing it to me, she took it right back and laughed, said she decided it was OK like it was. After a few months, Lewis came back to Edgefield to visit again and this time he asked Mattie to marry him and go back North with him. I was happy for Mattie but that was going to leave Mae with nobody to help her. Lewis came over to our house one afternoon when I was there. Mae was in the yard doing laundry and Mattie was still at her job in town and asked me, "Can I talk to you about Mae?"

I told him, "Mae can't live all by herself. She can do most things, but I don't know if she'll be all right all alone. I'm gonna tell Willie she's gonna come stay with us."

Lewis told me, "I was hoping she could stay at Mama's house with her. My mother can't hear or see too well anymore, and I think, with each one of them helping the other, they might be happy living together here on Brooks Street where they both feel at home."

I realized that was as good a plan as Mae living with me and Willie Clark's people, people she didn't know at all, when she had known Mrs. Hardy her whole life. We got everybody together that evening to talk about it. Mrs. Hardy was satisfied and happy and Mae was accepting of the change that was going to take place in her life.

The situation with Mattie and Lewis and with Mae and Mrs. Hardy took a burden off me really. But in my own life, things were not so peaceful. By then seem like Willie was smoldering inside. There were days I felt like he hated *everybody*, and not just white people like Strom Thurmond but his own people who endured what they went through without getting angry like he was. He got more bitter every day and he was not at peace knowing about

Essie Mae. He said, "Don't you know his people been doing this to us forever? Don't you know his own granddaddy had two sons by one of his slaves! Look around at all the colored people with light skin! Where you think that came from?" Sometimes he said things made it seem like he thought it was my own fault. Like "Why you didn't fight? Why you didn't holler? Why you didn't quit working there! You wanted him to do that or something? Answer me!"

"How dare you ask me that! Willie, I was a child. I was weak from my mother just dying! You could *never* understand! Just because I didn't fight doesn't mean I wanted it to happen! What do you think I am?" I screamed until I collapsed. He did not help me up.

———◆———

Mrs. Alexander, my dreams are getting so hard to escape, especially the bad ones. Last night it was a girl and her sister laughing and walking in front of the courthouse in Edgefield. They're carrying a brown and white puppy, headed to Reel's store, talking and planning what they are gonna buy with a dollar they have saved up. They don't see a large reptile slouching toward them and they don't step off the sidewalk to let it pass. When it gets to them and they look up still laughing, it snarls and screeches at them until the whole town hears and gathers around those sisters in a circle. The one with the puppy squeezes it so tight it yips. Two men take her and nail her ear to a tree in the middle of the square. Take a hammer and a nail and one of them holds the girl while another one grabs ahold of her ear and drags her to the tree and presses her ear to the bark while the first one drives a nail through her ear and deep into the wood. The other sister stands still and watches, unable to move or speak.

A different doctor came to make rounds here today. He took my temperature and lifted my wrist to count my pulse. The nurse helped him raise me up and pull up my gown for him to listen to me breathe. His hands felt good on my back, cool and smooth. He smiled but had nothing much to say. He asked the nurse to get another pillow to put behind me to help me breathe. When it gets hard for me to breathe, I always think about my mother.

Chapter Sixteen

When I married Willie, I brought what clothes I had and the money I'd saved to get us all to Philadelphia, but that is all I took from home. I got work two days a week as a maid and sewed at night until it got too dark to see to make the small, even stitches I was proud of. I was making on average one dress a week for somebody in Edgefield — colored women and white. My money was growing slow but sure and one night after supper when everybody but us had gone to bed, I told Willie, "You know I been saving money for a long time, and I've about got enough for us to go to Coatesville like we planned. There's enough money for us to get a place and settle in before you have to get a job. We need to talk to your folks and let them know."

Willie looked out toward the field and started hedging, "I ain't sure I can leave Daddy right now with all the work needs to be done here. Somebody's got to see things get better down here," and so on. Willie started getting up earlier to go out to the field, staying out there later in the evenings, like he was maybe proving to me how much work there was for him to do. He started helping his daddy with the ledger where they kept track of the farm expenses and the income they got from crops and livestock they sold. I knew it might take some time to get Willie used to the idea of leaving, but I couldn't accept that he would not go. But I began to see it: he wasn't going.

I asked him, "Can't your brothers do what you do? We can come down on the train to visit. They can come see us. You the one always preaching about how bad things are down here. You said before we got married you would go with me!"

"I never said that. You heard what you wanted to hear."

"You said we would work things out!"

"I never said I would go to no Pennsylvania!"

It wasn't long 'til I came home from work one day and found Willie sitting at the table smiling and in front of him was a small box and a sewing machine. I had never dreamed about getting a sewing machine and did not know how to work one. My aunt Lucy had sewed everything by hand and that was the only way I knew to sew. But this machine attracted me like a magnet. I sat down in front of it and touched it — it was beautiful — and ran my finger over the gold letters on the shiny black finish and the fancy gold decoration, S-I-N-G-E-R. I followed the loops and hooks where the thread would go 'til it reached the eye of the silver needle and felt the sharp tip with my finger. As I pulled my finger out from under the needle, the tip of it snagged the fleshy part of my fingertip and a drop of blood oozed out. I sucked it off quickly and Willie got down on the floor and put my foot on the treadle and said, "Pedal on this thing here." I did, and the needle went up and down by itself. The faster I pedaled, the faster the needle flew. Willie's mama was as excited about the machine as I was. Even Jerry was amused by the shiny new "toy" that hummed as I worked the pedal with my foot. Then Willie handed me the small box. Inside was a very stylish bracelet made of seven square pieces of butterscotch-color stones-- not all the same shape exactly. The pieces were held together by thin, gold wire that wound around each stone and then joined the pieces together like a chain. Willie put it on my arm and fastened the clasp. I knew he just wanted to make me happy, make me want to stay. I didn't want to spoil the night for everyone else, so I tried to seem happy.

After Willie went to sleep that night, I laid awake thinking about how much faster I could finish a dress with this machine and how much more money I could make sewing for people as long as I got the orders. Maybe I could quit my maid job and just sew. I had to admit I was glad to have the machine.

I was too worked up to sleep, so I slipped out of bed after Willie started snoring and his lips started puffing in and out like they did. I opened the chifforobe door, reached back behind our clothes and got my money jar. I opened it as quiet as I could and stuck my fingers down in there, pulled out the money and immediately knew something was wrong. It didn't feel right in my hand. I lit a lamp and placed it on the floor to keep from waking Willie. In a panic, I dumped the money into the lap of my nightgown. I counted. Most of it was gone. I kept reaching into that empty jar with my whole hand like that money was somehow stuck over to the side or something. But it was gone. I couldn't believe it. Nobody in Willie's family would have taken it. I knew that Willie took it and used it to buy that sewing machine. I felt sick. My head pounded and I could hardly breathe. I was awake in disbelief the rest of that night.

Next morning, first thing Willie did was get my hand and pull me toward him, but I pulled away and got out of bed and started putting on my clothes.

"What you doing, baby?"

I whirled around and told him, "Getting away from the man who stole from me."

First, he was too surprised to say anything, then he said, "Wait, baby, you got to listen! I just borrowed it! It'll help you make more money and quicker. I could have paid for it myself in another couple weeks, but when it came in at the post office, I didn't have the cash right then. I'll get your money back to you. I thought I could do it before you knew I had used it. I just *borrowed it* for crying out loud!" I bolted toward the door. He jumped up and reached for me but got his foot caught up in the sheet and stumbled and fell forward. He grabbed my arm as he was falling and pulled me down, too, and I hit my head against the wall.

About this time his mama ran in there yelling, "Slow down! Slow down!" and Willie started jerking his pants and shirt on and stomped out the house, brushing past his mother. His mama helped me up and helped me to the bed. Genie was nothing but kind to me ever. She sat down by me and held me. She couldn't help but to have heard us fighting.

I started sobbing to her and saying over and over, "I just need to go be with my child. Willie doesn't understand. I just need to be with my child."

Genie told me, "Y'all can work this out. I know y'all can if you both just talk it through."

"Willie said he would go with me to Pennsylvania, but now he says he can't leave his daddy with all the work on the farm. He won't leave this land. He wants to change things down here."

"I know you want to go, Carrie. I don't want y'all to go, but I know you want to really bad. We never have talked about your little girl, but I can imagine how much you want to get to her. It's a situation where there's not an easy answer."

"Genie, I might not should've married Willie. He needs somebody who can stay here, live here with all y'all and give back as much as they get. Me, I feel like I'm taking from the family, causing tension. I didn't know that would happen. My baby was torn away from me when she was six months old. My heart is stretched from here to Pennsylvania where she lives with my sister. Every year that passes is one less year I could still be a mother to her. He had told me he would go with me."

"I couldn't have stood to lose one of my babies either. Willie shouldn't have used your money without asking you. He's a good man. He thinks he's doing the right thing, but sometimes he don't give anybody else credit for doing what they think is the right thing. I just hope you won't stay mad at each other. I hope y'all can work things out."

Genie hugged me and cupped my face in her hands like Mama used to. I cried then for so many different reasons. Genie helped me up and to the back door. I walked to the far end of the yard where the outhouse was and stepped inside and closed the door where it was hot and close and turned the latch, sat down on the wood seat with my elbows on my knees holding my head in my hands.

It took a few days of all of us not saying much for the tension of that episode to die down. When we started talking again, Willie told me one night, "I'm sorry. I promise I won't ever do anything to hurt you again." Then he handed me a roll of bills. "I've got your money back. Go put it back in your jar."

I told him, "I just need to make up for the time I've lost with Essie Mae. Up there you can get a job and forget about lynchings and Jim Crow and all the things that eat you alive!"

"I hear things up there are no better than they are down here. Folks think they gonna be treated good up North, but they get there and it's the same as here. Besides, I can't stop thinking about what Thurmond did to you and how he ain't done a thing to help feed and raise your child! His child! I bet him or his daddy one paid somebody to get her out of Edgefield so he wouldn't have to mess with either one of you or have you make trouble! He nearly ruined your life and I'm trying to help you get some of it back but you're too dumb to realize it!"

That was the most I've ever been hurt by somebody I cared about. I'll never forget Willie saying that as long as I live. A slap in the face would have hurt less. I sat still on the side of the bed with my hand on my heart. I thought my heart would break. Suddenly we were right back where we started. We threw another match on kindling.

"You got to go to him and ask for the money he should have given you to help take care of that baby. If he had, you wouldn't have had to let her go. He's shooting for a big career in politics, and he don't want anything coming up about a colored baby that would hurt him! You could get money out of him just to keep quiet! Don't you see he *owes* it to you? If you would just think right, you would see this."

"I didn't let her go because I needed money. I let her go because I got scared for her life!"

All this talk made me feel sick, but by then Willie had got obsessed with me going to Strom for money. But it wasn't the money Willie wanted. He saw an opportunity to get some kind of revenge, but I would have to be the one do the work to get it. I got thinking if I did get money from Strom, I could leave Edgefield and go to Philadelphia and be with Essie Mae and Mary once and for all. Willie could go with me or not.

But about this time, I started getting big again. I got on my knees and begged, *begged* God every night for weeks that I would not have another baby. God, please don't put that on me now. But Mama had told us God doesn't answer your prayers if you are afraid. It meant you didn't have faith if you were afraid. Willie, though, he was so happy about the baby and so was his family. It would be the first grandchild for Genie and Jerry.

I kept busy sewing, and I would visit Mae and Mrs. Hardy back in Old Buncombe about once a week. Mae would usually be sweeping the yard or boiling clothes in a pot in the yard or cooking something. Mrs. Hardy couldn't see much at all, especially by late afternoon when daylight was fading, but Mae was her eyes now. Mae "read" the Bible to Mrs. Hardy mainly by Mrs. Hardy telling Mae from memory what the words said when Mae got stumped. Mattie had married Lewis, and they were living up North and Mae told me Lewis sent his mother five dollars every other week. They were doing OK.

Then time came for the baby to come. It was a boy. We named him Willie Clark, Junior. That was 1932. I was almost twenty-three years old. I was in labor for three days. Willie got up and down, up and down, all night and all day, praying and cursing, and I lost so much blood when he was finally born and I got so weak in the days that followed Willie took me to a doctor who told me to rest and eat calf's liver to build my blood back up. That very day Willie's daddy slaughtered one of their calves so I could eat the liver. Willie's mother helped take care of the baby until I got stronger. The doctor also told me I shouldn't have any more children or it might kill me.

Willie Junior brought pleasure to all of us back then — me, Willie, Willie's daddy and mama. Willie's brothers and sister adored him. Main thing was he loved to make us all laugh. From time he could crawl, he liked to hide behind a chair or a doorway and wait for somebody to call out "Where is Willie!" Then he'd poke his little head around, mouth wide open with two baby teeth on the bottom, and squeal like he had put one over on all of us. And he was a cute baby. Still is a good-looking boy. The tension between me and Willie eased up some when Willie Junior came along. And Willie could shut out the outside world.

One Christmas when Willie Junior was about four, Mama Genie had cooked a big breakfast for all of us. Jerry had cut down a cedar tree and Genie had decorated it with popcorn and cookies. Willie and his daddy had made a wagon for Willie Junior to be from Santa Claus. Jerry liked to go around the table having everybody answer a question, like what they were most thankful for or what the best thing they had done that year was, things like that. That morning we had got to talking about dreams and all of us started telling what we had dreamed the night before. It got around to Willie Junior 's turn. He sat there a minute then piped up, "I dreamt a stick!" It seems so silly now, but that morning he made us all laugh so hard, and "I dreamt a stick" became our answer any time the subject of dreams would come up.

While all them were laughing and happy — and I didn't blame them a bit because they were all together and healthy — I thought about my family. I thought about one Christmas back home in Edgefield. It was before I ever left for Augusta. Late December down there it gets cold and the sky looks like snow some days and the air is damp and sharp. On Christmas Eve Daddy took Mary and me with him to Reel's General Store to buy candy to put out that night from Santa Claus. Mr. William Reel knew Daddy since that's where Daddy had credit. Mr. William scooped some of those shiny hard candies out the jar into the scale with one hand while he shook open a paper sack with the other hand, then slid the candies from the scale into the sack. While Daddy got some change out of his purse, Mr. William scooped up two more pieces and offered one each to me and Mary.

"Y'all gals been good this year so Santy Claus will come see you?"

We didn't say anything 'til in one motion, Daddy put his hat back on with one hand and closed his other hand around top of my head and turned my head toward Mr. William. "What y'all say to Mr. William?"

"Thank you, sir," we both tell him. When we got out the door, Mary handed me hers because candy would make her teeth hurt.

That night, Mama spread the candy out on the table. I hugged Mary and thought about how Mattie and Mae would wake up and believe Santa Claus came in the night. Willis was just a baby, too young to know about Santa Claus, and Jim hadn't been born yet. I remember looking over at Mama and seeing her eyes were soft and wet.

Thinking about that time way back, I looked at Willie Junior and thought about how he was so happy and so loved. Then I thought about Essie Mae and wondered what she was doing up in

Coatesville and if they were having a good Christmas and wishing I hadn't lost so many Christmases with her. And I hurt thinking about that long past Christmas with Mama and Daddy and my brothers and sisters.

Willie Junior is fifteen years old now. Much as I didn't want to have another child, he has been a blessing. He'll be coming here to see me pretty soon, Mrs. Alexander, and I hope you can meet him. He goes to school in Chester where he is president of his class. Things didn't start out as good when we first got here though. The teacher he had that first year couldn't understand Willie's Junior's Southern way of talking and she labeled him as retarded. She made the white children in the class sit next to him for punishment when they misbehaved. He suffered that year, but he stood it. And the next year he had a good teacher, and she recognized he was real smart, and things have gone good for him since then. That first year was bad though. You'll meet him soon.

————— • —————

He's fifteen? I lost a baby who would be fifteen if he had lived. He was born premature and lived only a few hours. It's a pain I hardly ever share with anyone, Carrie. But within five years after losing that little boy, we welcomed two baby girls who are almost teenagers now and who make our lives complete. I don't think I could bear it if either of them were to be taken from me.

Shall we stop here for the day, Carrie? So far, I've made meticulous notes and want you to rest assured that your story is safe with me. I have a meeting tomorrow, but I'll come here after that. I hope you sleep well. Can I get you anything before I leave? Carrie?

Chapter Seventeen

WILLIE, JR.'S BIRTH BROUGHT SOME PEACEFUL YEARS BETWEEN Willie and me, but there was a longing in me that would never go away. Maybe Willie felt it. Maybe he thought it would help me get past that longing if I confronted Strom. Whatever the reason or reasons, he began pressuring me to go to Strom. Essie Mae was six years old by then, almost six years since I'd seen her. In one of her letters, Mary sent me another photograph of Essie Mae. She had on a little plaid dress — I know Mary must have made it — with a round, white piqué collar and white cuffs at the edge of the puffy sleeves. Her hair was plaited into three pigtails and her lips were parted just enough to show there was a gap where she had lost her two front teeth. Essie Mae was looking straight at me and very serious in that photograph. She looked like him.

By this time, Strom had served as the Edgefield Town County Attorney and practiced law in his daddy's office next to the courthouse in Edgefield 'til he was elected to the South Carolina State

Senate. Then his daddy died. That was June of 1934. I was in the kitchen helping Willie's mama when one of Willie's brothers came in to eat, talking about how Mr. Will Thurmond had died at his home. I didn't look up but hearing that news stopped me cold there where I was washing dishes. I felt Genie look over at me.

A couple days later the funeral was held at the Willowbrook Cemetery near the First Baptist Church, and Willie insisted we go into town to see what all was going on. Before we got right downtown, we could see cars parked bumper to bumper anywhere you looked, come for the funeral. Men dressed in suits and hats standing around on the sidewalks and on the square across from the courthouse talking. Other men in overalls standing on the sidewalks a little farther down the street. The only store open was Reel's and we went in for Willie to buy some snuff and give us a reason for being there. While we waited to pay, we heard one man telling about how Mr. Will Thurmond had given his family credit when their crops did poorly and how later he sent them a week's worth of food when their little boy died. Then another man calling him a son-of-a-bitch for suing his brother and ruining him. There were a few colored people came out to pay tribute, too, for one reason or another. Most businesses in town had shut down for those few days, and you could feel a dead weight, together with a kind of live energy, mixed in the June heat there in Edgefield. I felt a weight lifted *off* of me just knowing he was dead.

Looking back at everything, I see how so many events of that time were connected. Like this, for example. Wasn't long 'til I got a letter from Mary. When a letter would come from her, I didn't open it right off. I would wait until we had finished supper and take it in our room and close the door. I'd slip my finger under the flap with my heart excited and aching at the same time for news about Essie Mae. This time though, the news was about Mary: John Washington had left her. She said he had been drinking and most of his money went to liquor. One day he walked out. Mary wrote: "Can you send some money to help me out until I can get work and find someone to watch Essie Mae in the afternoons after school? We going hungry if something don't turn up soon. Love, Your sister Mary." Where would I get money to help Mary? We weren't going hungry, but we didn't have much cash money. We had spent my savings after Willie Junior was born and I wasn't able to work. This news came as a shock like so many things do.

When I told Willie Mary needed money, he saw that as another good reason for me to go to Strom. "Look. Mr. Will is dead. Mary needs money to take care of Essie Mae. You'd be a fool not to go do it now. If you care about Essie Mae, you will do this. You owe it to your sister and to your daughter."

Was Willie right? Was I failing Essie Mae and Mary by not standing up and demanding help? How could I *demand* anything? And what if I stirred up something that would come back to hurt me or Essie Mae or even Willie or Willie Junior? I agonized over what to do. The pressure from Willie was stressful, but, at the same time, it began to seem like he was right; I did owe it to Mary and Essie Mae to get help if I could. I dreaded to do it, but I said I would go see Mr. Strom. After making that decision, I could hardly eat or sleep for the knots in my stomach. I was afraid again, so there wasn't any use for me to pray.

Willie and I took the wagon into town soon after that to see if we could figure out a time when Strom was usually in his office. We saw him from a distance late in the afternoon leaving the courthouse and going just a little ways down the street into the white cottage that was his law office. Willie said, "That's when you going to knock on that door and do what you need to do. What you *have* to do."

So, I was actually going see the man who, just days after my mother died, had altered my life forever. When he took me out to that shed, he didn't see a girl who had just lost her mother. What did he see in me? Did he not think I had human feelings? As I thought about what happened to me that day, I found myself feeling closer to Willie. Like we were now on the same side. That helped me move forward with a purpose. I put on the best dress and shoes I had and brushed off a pocketbook Willie's mama had given me. I was ready to go, thinking like it's now or never.

Willie took me in the wagon and hitched it up on the edge of town to wait while I walked the rest of the way down Buncombe Street to Strom's office. I felt like hundreds of eyes were watching me. Four or five steps led up to a door on each end of the building -- one door to Strom's office and the other to another lawyer's office. We had seen Strom go in the door on the right. I didn't know would he let me in, would he know who I was, or what, but I knocked on the door. Seemed like forever before I heard noise inside that sounded like papers rustling and the legs of a chair sliding across the floor, then footsteps. Strom opened the door and there I stood. He said nothing for a few seconds then, "Can I help you? Won't you come in." Then I was inside. The smell must have been a mix of old leather-bound books, ancient paper files, wooden furniture several generations old. I panicked. I didn't know what to say, I just wanted out of there. I focused my eyes on his college diploma framed, hanging on the wall behind him until I got my bearings.

"Good afternoon, Miss. Carrie, is that you? I'm mighty surprised but pleased to see you. Have a seat." I let myself be guided to a chair and he went around and sat down across from me. He fiddled with a silver letter opener and asked me, "How've you been gettin' along? What have you been doin' all this time?"

"I'm married now, and I have a baby boy. Named after his father."

"Well, now, that's wonderful, Carrie. Now, what can I do for you? Is there some kind of trouble?"

I started slow: "Mr. Strom, I had my first baby nearly ten years ago. Your sisters came for a little while and helped me with food and gave me a little money."

"Yes. My sisters. They very kind ladies."

"Yes. Then, I guess you know, somebody came and took my baby and took her to my sister in Pennsylvania." He blinked. Showed no surprise or any other kind of emotion. Neither one of us said anything for a bit.

I took a breath, "She's almost ten years old. I don't see her, but my sister writes and tells me all about her. I've been trying to get up there to her, but things have happened, and I haven't got there yet. But now my child needs help. My sister needs money. Her husband left her, and she needs money right now so they can eat and stay in their house. And I must help her." My heart beat faster knowing what I had to say next. "I haven't ever talked about this — about my daughter — to anybody except my family, but I will have to ask for some help somewhere else if you won't help me."

He sat there fiddling with the letter opener, not saying anything, then, "Carrie you don't look a day older than when you helped my family back in those days. Course, you were pretty then but you even prettier now."

When he reached across his desk and pressed his fingertips down on my arm, I drew back like a snake had struck me. He withdrew his hand and just said, "Why don't you come back this time next week, and I will see if I can have somethin' for you. It was wonderful to see you, but I'm gonna have to ask you to leave now because I'm expectin' a client," and he was standing up and moving toward the door to get me out. I was so overcome with emotion that I can't remember what I might have said; I just left.

Willie was waiting in the wagon, and he couldn't get me in quick enough to ask what had happened. When I told him I had to come back in a week, he wasn't thrilled, but he nodded like he was satisfied that something was gonna come from that visit. Myself, I felt relief. I felt no joy, but I didn't feel bad about what I had done. Soon as we got home, I wrote Mary to tell her I would be sending her some money soon. That night I couldn't sleep for dreading to go back to Strom's office the next time but at the same time knowing I had to do it and knowing it would not be as hard the next time.

Over the next couple of days, the more Willie thought about the situation, the more confident he became that we had the upper hand. He told me, "He thinks he's got you under his thumb, but you and him are gonna change places! The bottom gonna be on top! The meek shall inherit the earth!"

The day I was to go back, Willie wrote something on a piece of paper, sealed it in an envelope, and told me to give it to Strom. What it was, he had written down two names: Mr. William Walton Mims and Mrs. Modjeska Monteith Simkins. Willie knew the last thing Strom wanted was any publicity to do with me, and that seeing those names would have an effect. You see, Mr.

Mims's daddy owned the Edgefield newspaper, and Mrs. Simkins was high up in the NAACP, the same lady Strom had worked with to get dental care for some of the colored schools when he was school superintendent down there. As a matter of fact, my aunt Bertha, who things had a way of reaching, had told me that Mrs. Simkins thought it was awful Strom didn't help when Essie Mae was born. Willie knew she was a colored woman with some power and that Strom would do what he had to to keep her or the Edgefield newspaper from putting out anything about him having a colored child.

When I got to his office, I raised my hand to knock on the door, but he opened it before I could knock. Standing there in his suit, smooth shaved and lean, he looked right at me and smiled like I was just a normal visitor to his law office. He greeted me using my old nickname, "Well good afternoon, Tunch. Young lady, you lookin' pretty as a rosebud again today."

"It's Carrie," I told him. He must have heard Mary call me Tunch back when I worked at his house. What was he trying to do using my childhood nickname?

"Of course, Miss Carrie!" When he put his hand on my elbow, I drew back again and he held both his hands palms up, eyes closed, head turned to one side and said, "OK, settle down, I know you always did like to play hard to get with me."

"I never played anything, Mr. Strom." I took my seat across the desk from him. He asked how I was doing and began some small talk and then said, "Now. Let's us get down to business here. I understand you need a little help. Is your husband not working?"

I said, "He is working on a few things," and I took the envelope out of my pocketbook and slid it across the desk toward him. Strom picked it up. "Let's see what you got here," and put on his glasses and slid the tip of the silver letter opener into the envelope, took out the paper, and studied it for a few seconds. He raised his eyes over his glasses and looked at me maybe surprised for a second, then took his glasses off and set them on the desk in front of him, smiled at me and said, "I see. Well, certainly we can work something out here, honey. I don't mind helping out your sister and your daughter. We don't need this situation to get complicated. Of course, I expect a promise from you all to keep all this private. Do I have your word on that? Things could get complicated if you break your promise."

"I understand." I held my chin up to one side and looked him in the eye.

"I will have an envelope for you here at my office on the first of every month and as long as we keep this simple, your sister and your daughter should be fine."

And that was that. Simple, really. No harsh words. No mess. No mention of the profound issue at hand — my life that was changed forever in one day by a powerful man. So, I would go downtown to his office once a month to pick up an envelope of money. I know there were people in Edgefield thought I went there for other reasons, and they spread rumors about me then and probably still do to this day, but I know the truth of why I went there. And you know, of all the times I did, only one time did he ask about Essie Mae, and then it was "How is *your* daughter getting along?"

Every time I got the money, I sent most of it to Mary. I put away some each time for my savings to go to Pennsylvania, and I gave the rest to Willie.

One of my last visits to see him was in 1939. By then he had been elected a state circuit court judge. I had been going to his office once a month for a while now to get the envelope. He invited me in like always, wearing a fine-looking suit and tie with his hair oiled and slicked back. He had cold Coca-Colas set out on his desk for each one of us. He smiled, "How do you do, Mrs. Clark." "Come. Have a seat over there. How's your family getting along? It's been real cold for this time of year, don't you think?" Then he said something I was not expecting at all: "You been comin' here every month now for how long is it? That's got to be hard on you, Carrie. To make things easier for you, I'd be happy to change our routine. How would you like to have enough money at one time to leave here and go be with your daughter and not have to come to me for this every month?" He watched to see my reaction. I was silenced for a few seconds, trying to process what he had just asked me.

"If you will leave Edgefield, I can give you a lump sum of money, enough for you to move to Pennsylvania, rent you a place to live, help yo' daughter out, and still have money left over to open yourself a bank account." He reached for a piece of paper and wrote something on it, folded the scrap, then pushed it across his desk to me. I opened it and glanced at the figure he had scribbled.

I had not expected that or planned for it, didn't know what to say, so I told him, "I'll have to talk to my husband and think it over and let you know next week."

He grinned when I said that. "That's fine." I guess he was amused at the thought of me asking him to wait on me this time. Then, "You give it some serious thought and I think you'll see it's to your advantage. You may not have another offer this good. Better not take too long though."

Then I was out of there, standing in the afternoon heat with sweat breaking out under my arms and my legs shaking, but I headed to where Willie was waiting for me in the wagon, my head down and my heart beating hard and fast.

On the way home I told Willie what Strom had offered me. Soon as we got back home, Willie got out a pencil and went to hacking the point with his knife, got out a tablet, and started figuring how Strom's offer compared to what we'd get if we just kept on going like we had been.

"Girl, that might sound like a lot of money to you, but it's not but what you'd get in two years' time. After that, you out of luck!"

I could sense this issue was about to cause some tension between me and Willie, so I took Willie Junior's hand. "Baby, come out here with me so Daddy can think some things over." Willie's mama followed us outside and got Willie Junior to walk with her down to the pasture.

Later, after Willie Junior had gone down for the night, Willie got my hand and led me outside to the front porch and we sat quiet for a while. It had cooled off a lot since that afternoon, or maybe I felt chilly from the tension between me and Willie. Then here it comes. He starts talking low at first. "Carrie, you know Thurmond's gonna run for governor. He won't want any rumors coming out about him having a colored baby. But right now, he's still a circuit court judge. Do you know that he just sent a colored man to the electric chair for raping a white girl?" By now Willie's voice is getting louder, "That son of a bitch sent a Black man to the chair for doing to a white girl the same thing he did to you! Let's see *him* with them leather straps across his chest while the man pulls the switch! Girl, how on earth can you endure it?" I had to get away, go back inside, feeling so conflicted by what Willie had said.

But it wasn't just the thought of Strom and men like him that tortured Willie; it was the thought of me and any of our own people who endured the way things were without feeling as Willie did. But Willie hadn't spent most of his life worrying about getting enough to eat like I had. His daddy owned the land he farmed and didn't have to give most of what he made to somebody else. They struggled when the boll weevil ruined the cotton, but they had food on the table even then. Willie didn't wake up and go to bed with his stomach clawing at him like we had. Being hungry can keep you from thinking about anything beyond how to get food for yourself and your family.

Who Willie was talking about that Strom sent to the electric chair was a man named George Thomas. A white girl in Georgetown, South Carolina, was raped right around Christmas time. The morning after, police arrested a colored man named George Thomas. While George Thomas was in jail waiting on his trial, a mob of white men came with guns and wanted the sheriff to turn him over. The sheriff didn't do that but instead slipped George Thomas out from the jail in secret and had him sent to the penitentiary in Columbia. For the next few nights, a mob of men swarmed through Georgetown scaring colored families until the National Guard got called out. When it came time for the trial, George Thomas's lawyer requested it be moved out of Georgetown so Thomas could get a fair trial, but Strom Thurmond, who was the judge, denied the request. At the trial, Thomas said he was innocent and that he had gone home drunk the night the girl was attacked, ate supper and went to sleep. His wife and son supported him, but the jury of all white men convicted him and didn't recommend mercy. That meant an automatic death sentence. Thomas's lawyer appealed the case to the state Supreme Court, saying he didn't get a fair trial because Thurmond wouldn't move the trial, but Strom made a report to the Supreme Court saying the trial didn't need to be moved. Strom didn't tell the court about all the people who came to the trial, so many folks you couldn't drive downtown for all the cars parked everywhere. So the Supreme Court wouldn't give George Thomas another trial, and he was electrocuted.

Willie stayed dead set against me taking the lump sum from Strom. He believed I should get what I was owed, which, he had figured, was a whole lot more than what Strom's offer amounted to. I could understand the math, that I was giving up a lot of money if I didn't keep going on the way I was, getting money every month. So be it. The next week I went to Strom's office and told him I would take the lump sum. He rose and from a cabinet, he took out a sturdy paper box, came back over and set it on his desk. With the back of his hand, he nudged papers away to clear a space between us. He took out ten stacks of bills. One at a time, he removed a rubber band around each stack, then, licking his thumb to separate the bills, he began to count out loud the same amount in each stack. He put the money back into the box, put the lid on, then pushed it across the desk to me, telling me, "I sincerely wish you good luck."

I looked him in the eye and told him, "Thank you."

I left his office on fire. At the bottom of the steps two men in overalls had to move aside to let me pass. I felt them turn and look at me when I went by. I was just a few steps away when they opened the door to his office and I heard them laughing and one of them saying, "Why, you old dog!" I know what they were thinking. And him chuckling, too, letting them think they were right, and telling them, "Just a family friend."

Let them laugh, I thought. Him, too. With the money I held in my hands, I was going to change my life. I was going to leave Edgefield and go find my daughter.

Chapter Eighteen

WILLIE AND I CONTINUED TO BE AT ODDS ABOUT ME LEAVING and he bet me that, if I left, I would be back in less than a month. But he wanted me to stay, even said he thought we should try to have another baby. "You know the doctor just being cautious so you can't blame him if it don't work out. You'll be Ok. You got your health back now. Have a baby girl and you'll be satisfied to stay here and forget about going to Pennsylvania. That's been keeping you unsettled long as I've known you. You need to get on with your life here. You got it good here, but you can't see it. Your sister's doing a good job raising Essie Mae. Plus, you sending money to help out. She'll know you didn't forget about her. Come on. You got one child by him and one by me. Have another baby so you have more from me than from him."

"That's perverted, Willie! You want me to have a baby, risk my life, so you can somehow beat him? You can't really mean that! Look. We go to Pennsylvania. We can send money back to your mama and daddy, come see them a couple times a year. They could come see us! We not moving to the moon!"

"You never had land or anything else down here, so you got nothing to lose. Me, I got this land my granddaddy bought after he was freed. He was a goddam *slave* and then worked 'til he could buy his own goddamn land! I ain't go' let that go! No way in the goddamn world I'm go let that go! Not for you or nobody! Why can't you see that?"

"I got a child up North and a child I'm taking up there with me. They the only children I will ever have! They're both my own flesh and blood, so don't tell me I got nothing to lose! Besides, if you cared more about your own child than about yourself and what *you* want, you'd come with me. You more like Thurmond than you know."

I had my reason to leave, and he had his reasons to stay. He was tied to that land his daddy owned and said it would be his someday and Willie Junior's after that, and he couldn't leave it, and he had to help his daddy maintain it. Said he would never turn his back on his family. Willie couldn't eat, couldn't sleep, the whole situation eating him alive. He had trouble sleeping even when he had worked in the field all day. He scolded Willie Junior one time when the child was crying with the earache, then hated himself for losing his temper with his child.

There just wasn't a way both of us could do what we had to do and stay together. I saw it and Willie did, too. He had to stay on that land, and he wanted to change things down there. I had to leave and be with my daughter who I had not seen in thirteen years. I couldn't go on talking about it and not doing anything about it. I knew I had to leave, and I would take Willie Junior with me. I went and bought the train tickets. Willie Junior was almost seven years old, old enough to be wondering what was happening to all of us but not old enough to understand it.

Willie's mama and daddy surely did not want me to take Willie Junior. Jerry had been letting Willie Junior walk with him behind the plow that spring and Willie Junior was excited about their crops that would come in soon. He was Jerry's shadow, sat on his lap after supper on the porch every night rocking, sometimes 'til he fell asleep. And Genie loved him with all her heart. She didn't cook a meal without making something special for him. When she made biscuits, she always made one shaped like a gingerbread boy for Willie Junior to butter and eat by himself. She read to him or told him stories every day. She would let him crawl in the bed with her and Jerry if he woke up in the night. It hurt me to think of taking him away from their love. I wondered if they would try to stop me from leaving with him, but they did not. I think Willie had convinced them that I would be back soon. He thought I would be. Willie's daddy couldn't understand how I could leave a life as good as I had there with them. I heard him ask Willie, "She think she's gonna have a life up there better than what she's got here?" Willie told him, "Daddy, that ain't it. She just can't get over losing that baby that's with her sister up North. She loves y'all. She just can't get over losing that baby." Willie took up for me. He could explain it to his daddy. He just couldn't accept it himself.

Next, I had the burden of going to tell Mrs. Hardy and Mae I was leaving. I took Willie Junior with me over to Old Buncombe to Mrs. Hardy's house. The smell of the hog pens was thick in the air that day — I knew that was something I would not miss when I left Edgefield. Mrs. Hardy was sitting out on the front stoop shelling peas and when she saw us coming, she set the bowl down and cupped her hand over her eyes to try to see who we were. When we got to the porch, Willie Junior reached out and put his arms around her. She cupped his face in her hands and smoothed her thumbs over his forehead and cheekbones. Her eyes were cloudy and wet. Her hair had turned white, and Mae had plaited it close against her head. I bent down to hug her. She smelled like soap and mint, and I breathed her in to try to hold her scent in my mind.

"Where's Aunt Mae?" Willie asked her.

"She walked down to Mr. Magwood's to check on him. He can't get around good now and Mae goes to help him get his breakfast and get him into his chair on the porch. She'll be back in a minute."

We looked up and there came Mae right then. Willie ran out to meet her. She hugged and kissed Willie and then took him around back to see her chickens that she took so much pride in. I sat down by Mrs. Hardy and asked her what she had heard lately from Lewis and Mattie. "They doing fine. Their baby boy is nearly two years old. Lewis still helps me out all he can. Sends me five dollars 'bout every other week. With that and what we grow and what you bring us, we doing OK." Mae and Willie came back around to the porch, Willie Junior holding a chicken in his arms like it was a cat.

I went on and told them, "Me and Willie Junior are going to Coatesville to where Mary and Essie Mae are. I wanted to come see y'all before we left."

"You planning on staying long?"

"If I can get work up there, we might stay on a while." I couldn't bring myself to tell them I planned to stay for good. "If I don't get up to see Essie Mae and get to know her soon, she's gonna be grown, it's gonna be too late."

Mae started twisting her apron in her hands. I hugged Mae and felt her tears on my cheek.

"Mae, if the time ever comes you need a place to live, say Mrs. Hardy gets tired of you, you can always live with me." I was trying to make things lighthearted. "As soon as I get work, I'm gonna send you what money I can regular." I pulled out a small roll of bills and tucked it into Mae's hand, trying not to cry.

Willie had already got up and gone out in the field when I woke up the next morning, the day we would leave. His daddy was going to take us over to Trenton – that's about seven miles from where we lived in Edgefield – to the depot. There we would board the Augusta to Charlotte line to Columbia, then take another train from Columbia to Charlotte. From Charlotte, we would go to Washington, then, finally, to Coatesville. Our departure time wasn't until six-thirty that evening. I laid out the best dress and shoes I had and packed my other clothes and Willie Junior's clothes. I packed the good scissors that Aunt Lucy had given me a long time ago, a small square slate that I'd had saved since I went to school in Augusta, and my letters from Mary and the pictures of Essie Mae. I put Willie's toys in a bag that he could keep with him on the train. I got out the bracelet Willie had given me the day he brought me the sewing machine and put it over with the dress I would wear on the train.

Genie was standing over the stove, cooking, making us a box of food to take on the train — biscuits, chicken, boiled eggs, fried peach pies. I put my hands on her shoulders, and she turned and hugged me. "I don't wish nothing but good for you, Carrie. I wish you and Willie could have stayed together. And I can't stand to think of little Willie leaving." That's when she broke down crying and I cried, too.

"Thank you, Mama. There wasn't anything you could have done to make things work out between me and Willie. We'll come back down soon as we can to see y'all. Willie Junior is sure going to miss y'all. You and Jerry have treated me like family from the start. So have Harold and Joseph and Dorothy. You got a wonderful family. I was blessed to be part of it. Willie Junior will always be a part of this family. I just hope Willie can find some peace. Maybe Dorothy can learn how to use that sewing machine. I won't be able to take it on the train."

I heated water to make Willie Junior some grits, got him up, and fed him. I was too nervous to eat. Genie stood behind Willie Junior and cupped his face in her hands. She knelt and hugged him for a long time. We spent the day trying to act like it was just a normal day, trying not to break down in front of Willie Junior.

We had an early supper, nobody saying anything much, and after supper, Willie went into our room and closed the door. I told Willie Junior, "You go in there and tell your daddy goodbye."

Willie began to fuss, crossed his arms, stomped his foot. "Daddy needs to come with us. Wait. Why ain't Daddy goin' with us? I'm not leavin' without Daddy!"

I told him, "Go on in, baby. Daddy's not going with us today."

He went in. The door closed. A few minutes later he came out crying.

Now it was my turn to go in to him. I slipped into our room where he was lying still in the bed. He laid there still, facing the wall. I know he was suffering. I went over to him and put a hand on his back and told him goodbye. Willie would not tell me goodbye.

For days, maybe weeks, maybe months, Willie had known I would leave. He had told me, "I'll come up there and get Willie Junior myself if you try to keep him there. You'll be back. You got to bring my son back to this family and this land." But I would not be back. I barely remember walking out the door, but come time to leave, I got my pocketbook and my bag of clothes and told Willie Junior we had to go. Jerry went on out the door and I followed with Willie Junior, heading to the wagon. I have never felt such heartache except the night they came and took Essie Mae. I heard somebody running behind us and turned around to see it was Willie. He grabbed me and hugged me so hard I couldn't move. Willie Junior shouted, "Daddy's going, too!"

Willie told him, "No, son. I'm not going. I just wanted to tell you and Mama goodbye one more time and tell y'all I'll see you before too long when you come back. Pop, I'll take 'em to the depot."

Jerry hugged Willie Junior, barely holding back tears. Then he turned to me and wrapped his arms around me. "You take care of yourself and the boy, Carrie. You know you always got a home here. You always be part of this family."

"Thank you, Jerry. Thank you for everything. You and Genie both."

He turned to go back inside, him and me both wiping away tears, and Willie helped me up into the wagon, lifted Willie Junior up onto the seat between us.

When we got there, Willie helped us down from the wagon and carried my bag into the long, wooden building where we saw waiting sections marked "Ladies," "Gents," and "Colored." We felt the ground vibrating and heard the loud rumbling of the train

— the Silver Meteor. Other passengers started getting up and gathering their things. We walked up the Colored platform and boarded the Colored car, the one right behind the engine, the one got the most noise and smoke. There weren't any luggage racks, so I crammed the bag with all our clothes and my box of food under my feet and settled in with Willie Junior close up next to me and we were on our way out. I looked out the window and saw Willie standing there. We locked eyes as the train began to move and I felt my heart breaking in two.

This was June 4, 1939, the day I left Edgefield. You ask anybody up here and they can tell you the very day they left home and came North. Willie Junior was seven years old. I don't understand how Willie could let me walk away with his son, though. Wasn't his own child more important than a patch of land? And did he really think he could change the world down there? He was older than I had been when Essie Mae got taken away from me. I was a child then. But Willie was a grown man. I guess he really did believe I would come back. While I had to leave to save myself, to be with my child I had lost so long ago, Willie had to stay, not just to save his land and his family, but to try to save all of us. Maybe it took as much courage for him to stay as it took for me to leave.

Chapter Nineteen

From the window of the moving train, I watched the sky growing dark as we moved farther and farther away. The rhythm of the train on the tracks hypnotized me while places I had known all my life slipped by — cotton fields and peach orchards, houses and farms. I thought about Willie Clark, about Mae and Mrs. Hardy. I thought about Mama and Daddy's graves. I thought about Strom Thurmond and his powerful job as circuit court judge. He was determining people's fate every day like he had mine.

Willie Junior was more interested in the inside of the train — the velvet seats and the windows with curtains you could draw back and forth, and the other passengers on the train. When Willie had to pee, we had to pass through the white car to get to the colored restroom. Willie held my hand and stumbled over my feet as we walked through the narrow aisle with the white passengers looking at us.

Back in our seat, Willie played on the floor around my feet with a toy horse and dog Willie's daddy had carved him as a going-away present, then watched out the window into the darkness until he got tired and leaned over on me and fell asleep. I rested my head on top of his little curly head and we stayed like that throughout the night, him barely waking to switch trains in Columbia, then again in Charlotte, still in the dark of night, and the train carried us north.

I never did go to sleep. I got to thinking about a day back when I was living with Aunt Lucy in Augusta and going to school with Velma. One warm day, hundreds of beautiful orange butterflies were lighting on the bushes in the churchyard. Velma called us all over. "These are monarch butterflies. Does anybody know what monarch means?" She always waited a minute to see if anybody could answer. "It's another word for a ruler, like a king or queen. These butterflies migrate north from Mexico every spring all the way up to Canada, but no single one of them makes the whole journey. A butterfly doesn't live but a few weeks, but in that time, it lays eggs that hatch into caterpillars that turn into butterflies and those new ones continue the journey, and on and on, until finally a generation of them makes it north. Sometimes it takes five generations of them to complete the journey."

"Where is Mexico?"

"I'll show you on the map when we get back inside."

"What's migrate?" So Velma explained that, too. "Do people migrate?"

"Some do," she told us, then ran her eyes over all of us like she was trying to figure out something.

I wish that I could thank Velma. Wish I could tell her I migrated north. I don't even know where she is.

As the train carried us farther from home, I wondered about what was ahead of us. I was anxious about getting work. I knew I had enough money to live on for a while, but I wanted work where I could use what talents I had. I could read and write. I could speak with good grammar if I needed to. I was a fast learner, and I knew I would catch on as well as the next person in a factory or a mill. And I could sew, thank goodness, or Mrs. Alexander, I wouldn't have met you and you wouldn't be here with me right now. Most of all, I wondered what it would be like to see my child. I would be seeing Essie Mae for the first time in thirteen years. Mary had written me that she had never given Essie Mae any reason to doubt that she was her mother. Would she believe I am her mother when we tell her? Was there a memory of me somewhere deep inside her? It was a thousand questions running through my head, but I was sure about one thing. I knew I had done the right thing by leaving.

We rode on and on for hours, ate from our shoebox, made trips to the colored bathroom, — me sitting up or leaning against the side of the car, Willie with his head on my lap and his feet curled up on the seat — and *finally*, we were almost there. Coming into Coatesville, I heard the porter announce we were about to cross the Coatesville High Bridge, so I woke Willie up to see it. You probably know that stone bridge with the four big arches that make it look like a giant caterpillar about a quarter mile long? When we crossed that bridge going over the valley of the Brandywine Creek, me and Willie both shivered when we looked down at the terrible water below us. The bridge is wide enough for four train tracks to run side by side. When we rolled into Coatesville at Third Avenue and Fleetwood Street that October afternoon, we were in for another surprise when we saw the two-story brick train depot that looked like a palace, so huge and grand, worlds away from the one-story, wooden Southern Station where we had started this journey. After that long ride, I unfolded myself, got ahold of Willie's hand, gathered up our belongings, and walked out onto the platform and down the steps into a foreign world with a smell of something harsh, like steel and smoke and raw, cold air. And the noises of traffic and steam coming from under the streets, whistles, sirens were like nothing I'd ever experienced. I looked for the colored signs but there were not any up here. I searched the crowd of people standing outside waiting for passengers to get off the train, and I saw Mary. And the young girl standing there with her I understood was Essie Mae. I pulled Willie fast down the ramp and next thing I knew Mary was hugging me through her heavy coat and wouldn't let go, swaying from side to side, and we were both crying, Mary saying "Thank you, Lord, thank you, Lord" over and over. Swaying in Mary's arms, I looked past her and saw Essie Mae again. She was smiling but detached, standing straight and tall in a brown wool coat with a velvet collar. She was beautiful. I looked into her face hoping that she was happy to see me, but I didn't see anything in her eyes, no sign of recognition. I don't know what I expected after all those years. Willie stood there shivering, his teeth chattering from the cold, when Mary grabbed him up and hugged him and told him, "I'm your Aunt Mary and you and your mama are coming home with me and Essie Mae."

The jitney cab driver Mary had hired, a colored man in a uniform and cap, was waiting for us with his car door open. He helped Mary up onto the running board and into the back seat first. Essie Mae stepped in next, then Willie scrambled in as the driver held my elbow as I got in. He checked to see we were all situated, shut the car door, and went around back to put our things in the trunk. There we were on our way, me on one side with Willie on my lap, Mary on the other side, and Essie Mae in the middle looking straight ahead. I couldn't take my eyes off her. She was tall like me. Her hands, resting on top of the front seat of the cab, looked like my hands, long thin fingers. Her skin was much lighter than mine, her hair thick and smooth. She had her father's profile.

We got to Mary's neighborhood, a place called Newlinville, onto a narrow street of houses lined up close together. With his cab left running, our driver got our bags out while Mary picked money out of her purse to pay our fare. We lumbered in tired, carrying our bags. Mary and I were laughing and crying, we were so overcome to be together again. When I held her face in my hands, she pursed her lips together to cover where she'd lost some teeth. I was sad that she looked older. I could see something of daddy in her expression.

Essie Mae took Willie under her wing. "Come on, I'll show you where to put your things. You can stay in my room with your mom. What grade are you in?" I stood taking in Mary's house. Although it was nothing to compare to the houses we'd both worked in back in Edgefield, it was much nicer than where we had grown up on Brooks Street. Inside the front door to the right was a small parlor with a fireplace and on the mantel were framed pictures of Calvin and Essie Mae. To the left was the kitchen. First thing I noticed was a red and white checked curtain over the sink and red and white linoleum squares on the floor. She had built-in cabinets with glass knobs, a gas stove, an ice box, and a white enamel worktable. Behind the parlor, a narrow hall led to Mary's bedroom. Upstairs were two more small bedrooms.

There was no sign of John Washington at all — no pictures, no pipes, no other possessions that might have belonged to him, and no clothes. I took my bag into Essie Mae's room. The room was small but filled with things important to her: a small desk with paper stacked up neat and a few pencils lined up next to her schoolbooks, a picture of her standing in the snow with Calvin, a picture of her with the members of the Public Speaking Club, and her chifforobe with her school dresses hanging neatly to one side. She lifted the dresses out and carried them over to Mary's room to make room for our clothes.

After a few days, Essie Mae relaxed around me. I could feel her watching me as I helped Mary in the kitchen or dressed or put on lipstick. She was not a talkative girl, looked like she was always thinking though, and when she looked at me, I wondered what was going through her mind. It would be a while before we told her I was her mother.

When I looked at her, I thought of myself at her age. She was fourteen years old. I was just a little older than that when my world was turned inside out. I said a prayer she would never have anything bad happen to her. I still pray that for her. For Willie Junior, too. I was about her age in Augusta when I started to like a boy for the first time. His name was Kenneth, and, like me, he listened to Velma read when some of the other children slept after lunch. He started staying after school with us to help Velma straighten up and clean the slates and desks. Kenneth was the only boy in the class as tall as me, and his britches legs hit about the middle of his shins. Velma sent us out together to shake out the rags we used to clean the chalk dust off our slates — I think she knew we liked each other. Both of us were too shy to do more than bump into each other on purpose going up the stairs and out into the church yard. I wondered if Essie Mae had a boy she liked. I wonder where Kenneth is now. He was smart and I wonder if he got to go on to school, if he stayed in Augusta

———◆———

I've crossed paths with so many people. When I was working on my degree, I interviewed a hundred families in the 29th Ward, all of whom had migrated north to find work. I was writing a paper on whether or not they could earn enough at their jobs, if they could earn a decent living. Some of them I'll never forget. Like you, I feel a loss in not knowing what happened to them, if they stayed here or went back South.

We lose everybody eventually, don't we, Mrs. Alexander?

Yes, or they lose us.

Chapter Twenty

You're here early today, Mrs. Alexander. Oh, your beautiful blouse! I remember when Mrs. Taggart put it on the mannequin and tied the bow at the neck to see if it was going to lay right. That became one of our most requested styles. Ladies liked how the silk fabric and the bow softened the look of a business suit. I still can't believe my luck at getting to work for Mrs. Taggart.

Mary had bought a newspaper, and I saw the help wanted ad for an experienced seamstress. I dressed and took the bus downtown to go apply for the job. I walked past the shop two or three times before I got the courage to go in. A bell over the door tinkled and Mrs. Taggart came out from a back room wearing this beautiful chartreuse dress with large wooden buttons, belted at the waist. It was the most modern dress I had ever seen.

She smiled and asked, "Can I help you?" as if maybe I was a customer. I didn't know it then, but she would help me in so many ways. She hired me and paid me well. If not for her, I don't know if

I would have got to this hospital when I did. And I surely wouldn't have met you.

Right off I noticed Mrs. Taggart had some stylish glasses she wore on a chain around her neck. The frames, she told me, were made from the shell of a turtle and turned up at the corners. She put the glasses on and looked at me carefully for a moment then said, "Tell me about your experience sewing. Then I'll need to see some of your work."

I told her, "My Aunt Lucy taught me to sew when I was a child in Augusta, Georgia. She could look at a dress on a mannequin in a store window and study it, come home and spread her cloth out on the table and cut out one like it. She sewed dresses for me while I lived with her. Sometimes I'd go to bed with her still up sewing and next morning I'd have a new dress to wear to school. First one she ever made me was a sundress that tied on the shoulders with a ruffle around the bottom of the skirt. I could spin around and make it twirl around my legs. Right away she started teaching me to sew. I got to where I did all the mending for her and everybody who boarded at her house."

"Did you just do mending, or did you ever make new garments?"

"Both. I could make a dress or a shirt, start to finish, time I left my aunt's. She taught me how to fold fabric to cut the pieces on the straight of the grain and how to arrange the pattern pieces to keep from wasting any cloth. Aunt Lucy showed me how to make all the different seams, a straight seam of course, a flat-fell seam, French seams. I know how to make a blind hem stitch and buttonholes, how to match plaids and make smooth darts. I sewed a wedding dress for a preacher's daughter back home and after other folks saw it, I got orders from other women both white and colored."

She smiled when I said that. I told her about the sewing machine I had learned to use. She handed me the coat she had been holding and said, "OK I need to see some of your work. Let's start with you mending the hole in the sleeve of this wool coat. I don't want to be able to see a single stitch."

Mrs. Taggart switched on a lamp and pulled a chair up for me. I took the coat and sat down at a table surrounded by bolts of fabric stacked and piled everywhere and garments hanging over doors and chairs.

"You select the needle and thread. I'll be back here working. You'll find thimbles in that dish — one of them should fit you. Let me know when you're finished." I looked through a box of spools of thread and found two or three that might do, then picked the one that disappeared into the color of the coat. Careful as I had ever been, I mended the sleeve where you couldn't even tell it had ever been torn.

"I've finished, ma'am." In a minute or two she came to look at my work, taking the sleeve in both hands and holding it up under the light. "That's very good, Carrie." Now I want you to sew darts into the bodice of this silk blouse on the machine." I couldn't believe it was the same model Singer that Willie had bought me, and I knew right away how to thread it. I felt a pang of gratitude toward Willie at that moment.

Mrs. Taggart put her glasses back up and leaned over my shoulder to examine my work. "Those darts are perfect!"

"Aunt Lucy taught me how to make them lie flat and smooth, all the way to the tip end."

"Your aunt must have been very talented. Did she sew for a living?"

"No'm. She took in laundry and rented rooms to boarders. She could do about anything though — sew, chop wood, slaughter a hog, put up vegetables, raise flowers. She was patient with me and took care of me like I was her own child from the time I was eight until I was fourteen. I went to school there, too. But I didn't get to stay long enough to finish school."

"Why did you leave if you don't mind my asking?"

"My father died, my mother got sick, and I had to go back home and work and help take care of my younger brothers and sisters."

"How is your mother? Better I hope?"

"No'm. She passed not long after I went back."

"Oh, I'm so sorry, Carrie. I'd like to know more about your family sometime. I've got one more thing I'd like to have you sew — this badge goes onto the sleeve of this army officer's uniform."

She couldn't even see the stitches I'd put in to sew the badge on. "You're the best applicant I've had," she told me. That made my heart soar. She said she could use me three days a week. It was late in the afternoon then and the bell over the door tinkled as a tall, handsome man came in. He wore the finest cut suit I'd ever seen, finer than anything I'd ever seen anybody wear back home.

Mrs. Taggart put her arm through his and looked up into his face. "Carrie, this is my husband, Hugh. Carrie is my new seamstress, if she will accept the position."

He said, "Nice to meet you, Carrie. I'm glad she's found someone who can help her out. She works too hard," then turned to her, "Honey, our taxi's waiting. If we don't leave now, we'll miss the beginning of the play."

"Carrie, I'll see you tomorrow at nine?"

"Yes ma'am, I'll be here. Thank you."

"Just a second, Hugh." She hurried to the back room and came out smiling, holding a pink scarf. She tied it close around my neck with a knot to one side, telling me, "This color will be good on you. This is the way ladies are wearing them in Paris. We want our clients to see we're stylish ourselves."

"It's beautiful! Thank you!" Mr. Taggart held the door for me to leave. Mrs. Taggart followed, locked the door, and I watched them jump into the waiting taxi. I walked away, wearing my pink scarf, feeling happy and proud. To work in a shop owned by a colored person was something I hadn't expected, and Mrs. Taggart was just so confident and stylish, like no one I'd ever known back home. In Augusta there was a section of businesses owned by coloreds that folks called the Golden Blocks. On one end was a colored theater, and on the other end on Gwinnett Street was the Penny Savings Bank and the Pilgrim Life Insurance Company. But there was nothing like that in Edgefield. I walked on toward my bus stop and on the way, I stepped into a ladies' dress shop and tried on a hat. Back home I could not have done that ever. I walked down the sidewalk looking in at the different businesses and stores — banks, a fur shop with mink coats draped around the shoulders of the mannequins in the window, a men's shoe store. I looked around at strangers who could not have cared less who I was, and I felt free and light. I stood tall and walked on to the bus stop to get my ride back to Mary's neighborhood. The sidewalk was crowded with all kinds of folks — old, young, white, colored, a family who looked Chinese, rich, poor, some in a hurry, some window shopping. A white man in a suit walked toward me on the sidewalk and before I knew it, I had stepped off the curb to let him have more room. The bus pulled up and let out a puff of black, strong smoke as the brakes screeched. The driver pulled a lever that opened the door and smiled at me as I climbed up to put my tokens in. When I put one foot up on the steps, a pain shot through my back and ribs. The pains were coming several times a day by then. As I looked around to find a seat, I thought, "You don't *have* to go to the back," but I took a seat about halfway back anyway.

That afternoon when Mary was at work, Essie Mae came into her bedroom while I was getting out of my work clothes. She watched as I untied my new pink scarf and hung my dress up in her closet. I moved some of Willie Junior's clothes off her bed for her to sit there and I let her put on some of my lipstick, then held up a mirror for her to look at herself. With her reflection and mine both in the mirror, Essie Mae looked from her own image to mine and back a few times and said, "Aunt Carrie, don't you think we look a little bit alike?" A lump formed in my throat. Mary and I had agreed Essie Mae had to know the truth about who she was and who I was, but I couldn't tell her then. It had to be when we were all together — me, Essie Mae, and Mary.

When Mary got home from work, I told her about our conversation and that I thought it was time we told Essie Mae. We worked together to get supper ready, and Mary told Essie Mae we wanted to talk to her about something after we ate. Willie was especially excited because his class was having an outing the next day to a museum in Philadelphia. He got ready for bed without a fuss. I cleared the table and Mary and I sat down, her on one side of Essie Mae and me on the other.

"What y'all want to talk to me about?" Essie Mae asked.

Mary started. "Well, baby, you know we all close in this family. Me and Carrie grew up together and took care of each other and of our little brothers and sisters from the time we were just children ourselves. Me and Carrie had a special bond. When our mama passed, with our daddy already gone, it was up to us to stick together to make sure the young ones got fed and taken care of. We had help from our neighbors and some of our kin, but we knew the one we could count on the most was each other."

Then I began, "I went to work for a family when I was fourteen, almost fifteen, right before our mama died. Just days after she died, I got pregnant." Essie Mae turned to look at Mary, drawing back in surprise. I kept going. "Around that time, Mary got married and moved up here. My baby was born and your aunts, Mattie and Mae, helped me take care of her, but then some other people got involved and thought my baby would be better off with Mary up here. I didn't want to let her go, but I was so young and didn't have a way to feed all of us. So they brought her to Mary. I knew I would come up here to be with Mary and my baby, but it took me a long time to get up here. Essie Mae, that baby was you. I never wanted to lose you. I hope I didn't lose you. Not a day went by that I didn't think about you and live for the day I could get up here and be with you."

Essie Mae didn't say a word, just wrinkled her brow, studying what she had heard, then she turned to Mary looking puzzled and maybe hurt and asked Mary, "Mama, why didn't you ever tell me?"

Mary told her, "I didn't want to do anything to ever hurt you. I didn't know if Carrie would ever be able to come up here. I didn't want you to think your mama didn't want you, so I just never could tell you. I don't know if that was the right thing to do or not."

It was hard for Essie Mae to know what to say. Can you imagine having to take that in all of a sudden like that?

I told her, "Mary had the biggest heart of anybody I ever knew. When they took you away from me, only thing that kept me from going crazy was knowing you were with her. I knew she would take care of you better than anybody else in this world, and she has. From now on, I'll always be close by to help you any way I can and show how much I always loved you even though I wasn't with you. I saved every word Mary ever wrote me about you and every picture she ever sent. I wore those pictures thin touching your face."

I expected Essie Mae to have a lot of questions. I expected her to say, "Then who is my daddy?" I guess it was so much to absorb that it took her a while for everything to sink in. Questions would come later. The only thing she asked was, "What am I supposed to call y'all now?" Mary and I looked at each other and the mood suddenly became lighter, both of us feeling relief to have that moment over with.

Mary said, "Just keep on calling us what you been calling us, I guess. Be hard to switch now."

It was during that time, though, I realized Mary was the one would always be Essie Mae's real mother. You can't make up for thirteen lost years. You can't expect a child to love you like a mother when she hasn't ever known you.

One afternoon Essie Mae came home from school running up the walkway to the front door waving some papers in her hand and shouting "Mama! Mama!" I almost fell over getting out the door to see what all the hollering was about. Essie Mae had been elected president of the Public Speaking Club. She was so happy and when I hugged her and told her Congratulations, she jumped up and down and said, "I can't wait to tell Mama. She will be so proud!" The rest of the afternoon while we waited for Mary to get home, Essie Mae watched out the window for her mother.

Me and Willie Junior had been living at Mary's for several months, crowded into Essie Mae's room and Essie Mae crowded into Mary's room. I felt like I needed to find a place for me and Willie to live that would be closer to where I was working but still close to Mary and Essie Mae. I would use some more of the money I got from Strom to pay our rent and, with the job I had got, I could give Mary some money every week, too. I accepted the fact that Essie Mae would stay with Mary, but I felt glad to know that, after all that time wishing for it, I was now a part of her life.

The room I got for me and Willie was in a tourist home called the R. L. Bennett Home for Women on West 2nd Street over in Chester. Our stay there was short, though, because they didn't ordinarily rent to women with children. Soon I found a tiny row house for us that even had an indoor bathroom. I felt proud to have a place of my own, but I worried about Willie staying home alone there after school until I got home from work. I could have found us another place, but I had to consider the amount of money I still had and not let it all slip out of my hands. What money I got from Strom had seemed like a lot at the time, but I knew I had to make it last. I thought about Willie and how angry he was when he looked at Strom's offer to me to take the lump sum. I had to do it though.

Not long after I started working for Mrs. Taggart, she moved me up to working five days a week, even sewing on some of her biggest projects. For the first time in my life, I felt satisfaction. I was living on my own up here in a new world with my two children. I was getting closer to Essie Mae. I was doing work I was good at and making enough money to live on. If somebody asked me what I did, I could say, "I am a seamstress." It was what I *was*. I was proud for the first time in my life. I was happy for a while. Leaving Edgefield was the best thing I ever did.

Chapter Twenty-one

Not long after I got up here, I got a shock from a story in a magazine called *Philadelphia Briefs* that Miss Taggart bought to read about movie stars and see what they were wearing — people like Jean Harlow and Katharine Hepburn. The stories in it were about famous people like the Lindbergh baby and scandals of some sort. I could hardly believe it one day when I picked up a copy and saw a story in there about Strom Thurmond of South Carolina and a woman from Edgefield named Sue Logue. The story said Strom and Sue Logue had been carrying on and he helped her get a job teaching school even though she herself hadn't even been to high school and another woman who applied for the job had graduated college. It said one time Sue and Strom were caught having relations right in his office at the school district. There was another part about her getting pregnant and going to a doctor to get an abortion, but the doctor told her she was too far along. Then it said that she tried to get rid of the baby herself and the baby, which was a girl, died. It showed pictures of Strom and Sue Logue together where they were smiling and looking like they were having a good time, one where they were standing next to a fancy car, and one taken from behind with them walking real close together. I wondered if anybody from Edgefield saw that magazine story and, if they did, what they thought about it.

Reading that article left me heartsick. Sorry for the lady who didn't get the teaching job — the one who probably deserved it. And sorry for the woman who did get the job, really. She looks tough in that picture, but she ended up losing her baby girl. Who wouldn't have a heartbreak over that.

Now comes one of the good things to happen to me up here, I met Roy Byrd. I had found a church I was going to and that's where I met him. I had tried a few of the big Philadelphia churches, but they were too formal to suit me, and then I found a Pentecostal Holiness church that a minister from the South had started in a storefront. They sang the hymns I'd grown up hearing and the congregation didn't hold back if they felt the spirit enter their hearts. Roy came and sat down on a chair between me and an older lady, smiled at her then turned and smiled at me. When it came time to sing, he opened a hymnal and offered me to hold half of it. When they passed the plate, he put in a dollar and pressed my hand back with my quarter in it and whispered to me, "My treat." I couldn't keep from smiling at him when he did that. When we walked out, he introduced himself and told me he hoped he'd see me at the Wednesday night prayer meeting. Of course, I went to prayer meeting Wednesday night. After, we went to a drugstore, and he bought us a Coke. Talking to Roy was so easy, and he made me feel comfortable from the very beginning. I guess the time I had with Roy was about the best time of my life.

He had come to Philadelphia from Kentucky when he was fifteen years old, so he was used to the North. He knew Philadelphia, knew a lot of people who liked to have a good time drinking and dancing and listening to music. He had a good job as a janitor at the post office. He believed Franklin D. Roosevelt was going to save the country and make life better for colored folks. Roy had a lot of anger, too, about the limits put on colored people, but he didn't let it eat him up like Willie Clark did. He told me that even though the North doesn't have Jim Crow, colored people have a hard time finding jobs, and when they do, they usually get the worst jobs and often get paid less than white people in the same position. He said the post office paid him half what they paid a white man to do the same job. Not only that, but the white man told Roy what to do. Roy said he'd say, "Boy do this, Boy do, that." But Roy had friends at the post office, colored and white, and he liked going to work. He had hope that the President was going to make changes that would give colored people more advantages than they had ever had before. He really believed President Roosevelt was going to equal out the lives of colored and white. I think that hopefulness took the edge off his anger.

On our first real date Roy took me to a picture show to see a movie called *The Grapes of Wrath*, best picture show I had ever seen. After that, we started going out almost every weekend. Willie Junior could spend the night at Mary's, and Roy and I could stay out late.

Roy often took me downtown to a club called the Downbeat where jump bands played 'til all hours of the night. The Downbeat was on the corner of 11ᵗʰ Street and Market, on the second floor above the Willow Bar and right near a fancy theater, the Earle. Musicians and singers playing at the Earle came over to the Downbeat between shows to hang around and play their music to a smaller crowd. That turned into our favorite place to go. I remember first time we stepped in there out of the daylight, I couldn't see a thing. I balked and Roy laughed and pulled me on inside where it was dark and smoky. You could smell cigarette smoke, musky perfumes, alcohol, and people all mixed together. Candles on the table gave off enough light to see people sitting around, just soaking in the night and the music and each other. Of course, I hadn't ever been anywhere like that before, and I felt so out of place. I felt like people were looking at me and could tell I was uneasy, but when Roy got ahold of my hand and pulled me up from my chair and started dancing with me, I forgot all about myself. His friends came over and clapped him on the back and hugged him. Two women came up and put their arms around him, one on each side, and asked him to introduce me. You could just tell people liked Roy. He ordered our drinks using words I had never heard, names of mixed drinks that turned out to be cold and smooth and made me feel relaxed. I watched Roy and admired how well he fit into this world which was new to me.

A jazz trumpeter named Dizzy Gillespie played there for weeks and I couldn't get used to the fact that colored and white people both were there enjoying it together like it was all the same to them. Nothing like that where I came from. The Downbeat is where I first heard Billie Holiday sing. We sat there listening to this young, talented girl, looked about the same age as Mae, and me just swaying in my seat with my eyes closed, feeling good from the cold drink I had in my hand, Roy with his arm around the back of my chair tracing my shoulder blade so light with his fingertips like he did. But when I heard her sing the words "Black bodies swinging in the Southern breeze," it hit me what the song was about. I came out of a lull. I looked around at the other people and wondered if they knew what she was singing about. The stories Willie had told me about people who were beat or shot or burned and then hanged came flooding over me. I thought about Willie Clark and my heart hurt for him and for all those people who had died so horribly. I respected Willie for knowing and caring like he did. And I appreciated him for making me aware of things beyond my own troubles.

The first time we made love, it was good. For a while. Roy knew how to do things I had never done before with Willie. Somewhere along the way, that old, powerful smell came into my head, the one all around me in the shed that cold morning. Every time, it would be so good for a little while until that smell came into my head and I felt like Roy could smell it, too, then the pleasure of it would be over for me. Roy would ask, "Baby, what's wrong? Something I did? Tell me." Finally, one night I told him everything, how I came to have Essie Mae, and how I got the money to come North. It felt good to be able to tell that to someone I trusted and who cared about me. The way Roy held me that night, saying nothing, asking no questions, just making me feel safe, I will never forget that.

One night me and Willie Junior woke up to drops of water plopping on us from where the roof had a leak. We had already been seeing damp chunks of plaster falling off the walls. Most of the time there wasn't any heat, so we kept our coats on day and night because it was so cold. When Roy offered to let us move into his place, I accepted his offer. When I told Mary and Essie Mae we were moving in with Roy, I told them we were most likely going to get married someday, but that was not exactly the truth. I was still married to Willie Clark, of course, but it was what I wanted, and it seemed to make us living together more respectable. Roy had said things made me believe we had a future together, but he had not asked me out right to divorce Willie so that I could marry him.

Roy took a liking to Willie Junior right off and bought him things and took him places. Willie walked around for a week like his arms and legs were suspended from strings after they went to the picture show to see *Pinocchio*. Roy took him around to some of his friends' places. He threw the baseball with Willie and took him to a few baseball games. Mrs. Alexander, you know last year that Jackie Robinson got to play major league. Roy would have loved to see that. Soon as he met Mary and Essie Mae, he invited them to do things with us, too, like go on a picnic or go to his house for a barbeque. I often thought about what Willie Clark Senior would have felt if he knew about me and his own son living with another man. I was sorry for what Willie was missing out on with his child, and I was sad that I was the cause of it.

———— ✦ ————

If you had stayed, you would have missed out on knowing your daughter. You had to choose. I'll be back tomorrow. I want to hear more about Roy.

Chapter Twenty-two

WHILE ME AND WILLIE JUNIOR WERE STILL STAYING WITH ROY, Mary got a telegram from our aunt Bertha telling us that our precious sister Mae had passed in Edgefield. Her dying so young — twenty-six, four years younger than me — was such a shock. It had been two years since I had seen Mae, but I'd been sending her money regularly. When we got more details, we learned she'd had the toothache for several days. The morning she died, she went out to sweep the porch, then came back inside to lie down. Mrs. Hardy went to check on her and found Mae unconscious. She stopped breathing without ever waking up. We would go back to Edgefield for Mae's funeral.

All that night I didn't sleep. Mae dying so sudden like that made me think about Willie Junior and Essie Mae. What were their lives gonna be like? Would they live long and have a good life or have a hard life? What about me? I knew by then that I was not well although I didn't know what was wrong with me.

With Willie Junior having his daddy's family to fall back on, I knew he would be all right if he needed help. But Essie Mae didn't have anybody but Mary and Mary didn't have any money. I wished Essie Mae could have a future after I was gone, that she could get an education and be a nurse or a teacher or something she would be proud of. I wished her father would help her. After all, her father was Strom Thurmond. The next morning., I bought train tickets for Mary, Essie Mae, Willie Junior, and myself to make the trip to Edgefield for Mae's funeral. The next available train was going to Columbia, so we would arrive there, then take a bus from Columbia to Edgefield.

We boarded in Coatesville early in the morning in July 1941. Essie Mae asked, "How old was I when I left Edgefield, Carrie?"

"You were six months old, so you're in for an experience you never had before." We were in a parlor car with colored and white people both, waited on by colored porters, but when we got to Washington, we changed trains at Union Station. That's where the cars were segregated and we had to move to the Colored car. Essie Mae looked to Mary for reassurance. "It's OK, baby, we'll be all right," Mary told her. Now there would be no visiting the dining room, so Mary pulled out our lunch we had brought in a shoebox and Willie Junior thought it was as good as having a picnic right there on the train. Our car smelled bad and the fans didn't work. Essie Mae was quiet from that point on. Mary could tell I wasn't comfortable and folded up her sweater to make a pillow for me to put behind my back. We rode all night for what seemed like a hundred hours until we were finally in Columbia.

Essie Mae was getting her first real taste of Jim Crow. Mary hadn't lived in the South for a long time herself, but she still knew what it was like. Essie Mae scowled at the colored signs and looked toward Mary with a puzzled and suspicious expression. As you know, Mrs. Alexander, there are no such signs here in Philadelphia. We had to sit behind all the white folks on the bus and when we stopped at the little towns between Columbia and Edgefield, if a white person got on, we gathered up our things and moved farther back, finally just going all the way to the back so we wouldn't have to move again. We all had to use the restroom at one of the stops, a country store where the bus had stopped for gas. Together, we climbed off the bus and found the restroom around back of the building. I went first to make sure it was OK. It was hot and nasty in there, and just as I was coming out to let Willie go in, a man came charging around there, spitting on the ground to one side as he bore down on us.

"What in the world y'all think y'all doing! You can't use this restroom. It's white only! You better get back on that bus while you can!" Essie Mae was horrified. She ran back to the bus — all the way to the back seats. I know Willie Junior will remember as long as he lives that once we got back, he wet himself right there in the seat, a dark circle spreading out on the front of his pants and then pee dripping onto the floor. He just couldn't hold it no longer. Mary handed him a handkerchief out of her pocketbook. He wiped at his pants, but it was no use. He couldn't even look up the rest of the way, he was so ashamed.

There was no bus station in Edgefield, so we got off in town at the square. Mary looked around and told me, "We back home, Tunch. You go' be OK?" Essie Mae stepped down into a different world from the only one she knew, into one with no tall buildings, no traffic, no crowds of people, no noise besides a couple of horse-drawn buggies passing by and distant conversations of a few clusters of men standing around here and there. Instead of the smell of factories, the sour smell of the hog pens was heavy in the humid air. Folks looked different down there, too, from their dress to their movements. A few men walking toward the court-house wore dark suits and hats; the men sitting on benches out in the square had on overalls. It was a Saturday, and some men had started drinking and talking loudly. When we got close enough to hear them, Essie Mae asked me if they had a different language from the white people in Pennsylvania. I told her, "Yes, they kind of do." She said not another word as we started walking toward our aunt's neighborhood, her trying to take in the place where she had been born. It must've been so much running through her mind, but she still didn't know the half of it at that point.

The town square had changed since I was last there. The same buildings were still there — the post office, the drugstore, the general stores, and the big courthouse with benches around the courthouse steps. That tall monument in the middle of town, the monument to the Confederate dead, appeared smaller than I remembered it. They had a new mayor named Harold Morris who had got trees and shrubs planted around the square and the whole area which used to be either muddy or dusty, depending on the weather, was now covered in grass. Same as when I came back from Augusta and the power lines had been installed, it was the same place, but some things had changed while I'd been gone.

We walked to our aunt Bertha's house carrying our belong-ings, people looked at us like they were wondering who we were. Finally, we got to Bertha's dusty road. When you walk in Bertha's house, you're in a hall they call a dogtrot because a dog could trot in the front door and out the back. In her parlor to the right of the hall, were a few pieces of beautiful furniture, like a velvet settee trimmed in wood, two matching tufted armchairs, and a small wooden coffee table with curved legs and a marble top. A lady she worked for had paid Bertha with furniture at times when she had run out of money, so Bertha's house had much nicer furniture than any of our other relatives' houses. Bertha came out slow, her fingertips touching the sides of her beautiful face, like she couldn't believe it was us standing there. She hugged me and Mary and Willie Junior, and then she stood back a little as we introduced her to Essie Mae. That's the first time I think we all together felt Essie Mae's difference, not just in her looks but in something about her whole self. Standing there in the middle of all of us, Essie Mae seemed foreign. Her skin was not nearly as dark as mine or as that of any of the rest of us. Her eyes, her cheekbones, her nose had some resemblance to our family but also had something we couldn't relate to. But her looks weren't the only thing that seemed different; something in her bearing, her posture, just felt different. They all were a little nervous around her and she was uneasy around them, too.

Soon as we hugged Bertha, me and Mary broke down from our grief over Mae, who had been the kindest one of all of us. Bertha told us more about how Mae died: "Mrs. Hardy said Mae had a toothache for a couple of weeks and the morning she died she woke up and her whole side of her face had swole up so that even her eye was shut, but she had got up and made breakfast for Mrs. Hardy, walked down to help Mr. Magwood, then went out to sweep off the porch. Mae came in still holding the broom but soaking wet, perspiration running down her face and not able to talk to say what was wrong. Mrs. Hardy said she felt Mae's cheek and it was burning up by then. She went to get some cool water and a rag, but when she got back Mae was unconscious. Mrs. Hardy worked to cool her down, but a few hours later Mae was gone. We think the tooth infection went to her brain." Mae's funeral would be the next day.

Mattie and Lewis came down from Chicago for the funeral and were staying at Mrs. Hardy's. Their baby was almost one year old, my nephew. When I held that little fellow close to me, I could feel my daddy's presence. First thing I thought of was I wished Mama was here so she could've seen him because he looked so much like our daddy, long, slender limbs and very dark skin. They walked to Bertha's that morning to go with us to the funeral. Mattie let me carry the baby and she and Lewis helped Mrs. Hardy make it to the wagon that would carry us to the church. Mrs. Hardy, small and frail now, broke down when I took Essie Mae to speak to her. "I can't believe this that tiny angel we had so many years ago. Thank the Lord I get to see you again, baby." Essie Mae smiled and let Mrs. Hardy hug her, put her arms gently around Mrs. Hardy, but like everything else in Edgefield, Mrs. Hardy was foreign to her, and nothing felt like a reunion for Essie Mae. Walking out to the cemetery, Mattie told me she and Lewis wanted to take Mrs. Hardy back home with them, but Mrs. Hardy hadn't told them yet if she would go.

This was Essie Mae's first funeral. Willie Junior's, too. We had it in the church our mother and daddy's funerals had been in. I had to shepherd Essie Mae and Willie both up to the front of the church to see Mae and pay their respects. It's hard to explain how Mae was beautiful. She would not have stood out in a crowd, but her face was smooth as the skin of a pear. She had large eyes that made her look surprised all the time when they were open, but seeing her there with her eyes closed, you could see how beautiful her eyelids were, transparent and fragile like Mae was. And Mae's eyes never got that hard look that I see in so many colored girls here in Philadelphia, the ones who have been made to grow up too fast and do whatever they have to to survive. Her fingernails were trimmed short, but even and smooth. She had never been out of Edgefield. She had never ridden a train. She never had a boyfriend or got excited getting dressed up and wearing high heel shoes or lipstick. She had never seen a city like Philadelphia with tall buildings or walked right into a store and tried on a dress or a hat like she was somebody. She had never gone to a club where whites and coloreds sat around at tables enjoying the pleasures of music and drink. She didn't know any other world besides the one there on Brooks Street. She had loved and been loved, though, by Mama, Daddy, all of us, and by Mrs. Hardy. She had loved helping others all her life even though her circle of loved ones was small. She had loved all the seasons, even winters down here where it gets freezing cold and usually snows a couple of times every year. She would see things in clouds nobody else could see. She would watch an ant drag a speck of food across the porch and move a stick out of the way for it. She had raised chickens and given them names and looked after them, gathering their eggs like she was finding treasures. She had loved Bible stories and hymns we sang at church. She laughed easy. Cried easy too, though. I couldn't believe she was gone.

After the service, we went outside to the cemetery where our mother and daddy's graves were. There was Mae's grave dug next to

Mama. I stared at the ground around their graves and wondered if I would be put in there when my time comes. While the preacher was reading "The Lord is my shepherd I shall not want," I got to wondering how much Mae's funeral cost and knew I'd need to talk to Mary and Bertha about us splitting it up. Mae hadn't paid into a burial society like Mama had, but I still had some money then and I could pay my part. We walked on through the valley of the shadow of death, to the wagon waiting to take us back to Bertha's house.

Back at Bertha's, folks from her church came in bringing food — sweet potato pie, fried chicken, greens, best food in the world. Bertha's Sunday School class kept a fund to help get food when one of their members had a death in the family, and often that was the most food the family had ever had at one time. Several ladies from the Sunday School class came to deliver it. I think some of them wanted to get a look at Essie Mae since she had been a baby when she left. Folks had not forgot about her and how she had got taken away. They all said how sorry they were about Mae and all of them eventually got over to speak to Essie Mae, look at her, see who they thought she looked like, I guess. They questioned her about school and about her friends, about her plans — everybody kind to her but still making her uneasy I could tell.

It was after supper time when they all cleared out. We talked about who all we had seen at the funeral. Then Bertha brought up a man who was there that she didn't recognize and was asking me and Mary if we knew who he was. Neither one of us knew him. I noticed he kept looking at Essie Mae, but then so did most everybody there.

"He told me he was sorry for our loss," Bertha said.

Essie Mae said, "He asked me how long we would be in Edgefield."

"What did you tell him?" I asked her.

"I told him we'd be leaving in a few more days. He took a gold watch out of his pocket and looked at it, then just smiled and walked away."

We sat and talked in Bertha's small living room for a while, then, one by one, we went back to take off our funeral clothes and shoes and get ready for bed. Once everyone else was settled, Bertha told me she wanted us to talk and she got us both a glass of shine her longtime boyfriend, Jake, had made and we went out on the front stoop in the cool night.

Most of the time through the days we'd been at Bertha's I hadn't thought about myself being sick if I was busy enough with something to occupy my mind, but when me and Bertha sat down out there in that dark quiet, my sickness came to the front of my thoughts and I wondered how it would end. When we sat down, Bertha put her hand on my belly and said, "Tunch, you sure you not expecting?" I told her, "No, I just swell a little from time to time. I ate too much of all that food today." I still hadn't told anybody I was sick but Mary.

"You want me to catch you up on Thurmond or you rather not hear about him no more?"

I told her, "I guess so," so she updated me on what he'd done since I left Edgefield.

She went back to when he had been appointed to the Senate Education Committee and Bertha said he worked to improve the schools by making the school year longer and raising teacher pay — white teacher pay, anyway. He had got concerned about communists getting into the school system to teach, so he wrote a bill where teachers would have to take a loyalty oath.

When Bertha was telling about Strom doing things to improve schools there, my mind went back to my cousin, Velma, and how she worked to improve education for colored children in Augusta. I went with her one time to the main school office in Augusta where we sat on a bench outside the building for maybe two hours waiting to get in to see the school superintendent. Finally, his secretary came out and told Velma, "You'll have to come back another day because he has another meeting coming up." But Velma told her, "We will wait until his meeting is over," and we did and the secretary soon told us, "Come on in now." Velma handed him a list of things she needed and told him out loud, too, she needed books and chalk, slates, benches. Since he hadn't asked her to have a seat, she stood there looking at him straight on. The man stood up and thanked her and kind of mumbled that he would see what he could do. I don't believe he had come up against a teacher as determined as Velma was to get what she needed to do her job. He sent word in a few days that she could go over to the white school and pick up the books they were throwing out. Those books were old and had pages torn out, but Velma got me and Aunt Lucy to help her and we drug a wagon over there and got them and Velma taught from them. Willie told me later about the Supreme Court ruling that said negro and white schools would be separate but equal, but the schools never were equal, and the white teachers got paid three or four times as much as the colored. Didn't anybody — including Strom Thurmond — care more than Velma did about improving schools.

Bertha told me Strom had personally met hundreds more people while he was on the Education Committee, so when one of the circuit court judges in South Carolina dropped dead of a heart attack, Bertha said Strom started politicking for that job and heading toward what he really wanted to do. He went all over the state shaking hands and getting votes and got elected as a state circuit court judge. Bertha said folks said he was probably aiming to run for governor.

"He's still got a reputation as a ladies' man more than ever." She picked up with the Sue Logue story, telling me more about that. Bertha knew more about Sue Logue than about her getting the teaching job. "Sue and her husband had a feud going with a neighbor named Timmerman whose mule had kicked one of the Logues' calves to death and the Logues wanted the neighbor to pay for the dead calf. When the neighbor didn't pay what the Logues thought he should've, the feud heated up. Sue Logue's husband went to the store Timmerman ran and got in a fight with him. Logue picked up an axe handle and started to hit Timmerman who pulled out a gun and shot Logue dead. After that, Sue and her brother-in-law put pressure on Sue's nephew, a police from up in Spartanburg, to hire a man to kill Timmerman. The FBI got called in and the nephew told them everything, and the cops went to arrest Sue. When they got out to the Logue house, Sue and some of her people were holed up inside the house and they shot at the cops and killed two of them along with another one of their neighbors. After the cops couldn't get her to come out, Strom walked up to the house with the pockets of his britches turned inside out to show her he did not have a gun, and he went in and talked her into surrendering. He walked her back outside to where the police put her in the car and took her to jail. Sue Logue was tried and found guilty of murder and sentenced to die in the electric chair, which she did. Here is the crazy part: Strom rode with her on the way to the penitentiary where she was on death row. The man who drove them there said they were hugging and kissing and all over one another in the back seat on the way there. Folks in Edgefield are hotheaded, don't matter if they are regular whites like Sue Logue and her husband or rich and powerful like Strom's daddy. If they think you've done them wrong, they might shoot you same as look at you. Nothing's changed much. Strom still goes after women." Bertha pulled herself up and had to help me get up off the steps, and we went inside.

Bertha poured us another glass of shine, which she said Jake made good money selling. It burned my throat going down, but sitting out there listening to Bertha and drinking Jake's shine made me feel things deeply. I felt grateful for Bertha's company and for all the friends who had come to honor Mae, sad for the loss of my sweet sister, lonely when I thought of Roy. I thought of the things I miss about Edgefield, about how it had been my home with Mama and Daddy, my sisters and brothers. I thought of Willie, what we once had. I thought of neighbors who had been kind to my family. I felt homesick for a place and time that I'd never be a part of again.

Have you ever been to Edgefield, Mrs. Alexander? It gets so quiet there at night, and you can hear crickets and tree frogs, maybe a dog bark way off. Sometimes the scent of a tea olive bush floats across and you think that must be what heaven smells like. Nights are dark enough there that you can look up and see a trillion stars if there's no clouds. It's beautiful, really.

It was after midnight when Bertha and I went back inside and told each other goodnight. Bertha laid down on the pallet she had made me and insisted I sleep in her soft bed. I still couldn't go to sleep for thinking about everything. It was hot in there and my head and back had got to hurting again. I thought about the man who came to Bertha's after the funeral who none of us knew who he was. All of a sudden, I panicked. What if he was there to plan some way to get rid of Essie Mae the same way they got rid of her sixteen years before. People with power and money can do things the rest of us can't. Strom Thurmond's people had plenty of power and money. Surely to God, Strom or his family wouldn't have anything done to hurt her, I know he wouldn't, but some of the people who wanted him to run for governor or some of his political enemies — no telling what they might do. My heart nearly pounded out my chest that night I got so scared at the thought that something could happen to Essie Mae.

Some people say everything happens for a reason. I don't usually believe that, but if I hadn't got so scared that night and if I hadn't been sick, I might not've done what I did the next day.

———◆———

Carrie, shall we save that until next time? Nurse is here with your pills. I'll be back tomorrow. I hope you sleep well.

Chapter Twenty-three

WE HAD BURIED MAE BESIDE OUR MOTHER. I WOKE THE NEXT
day with the pain you feel when you have lost a piece of your life,
one of your family, one of the people you truly love. Everybody
was quiet. Bertha had already got up and fried us pork and made
biscuits, and we had some of the food folks had brought over the
day before. Essie Mae and Willie Junior ate but I couldn't put
nothing in my mouth. I told them I was going to go downtown,
just look around, and went back to Bertha's room to get dressed. I
put my funeral clothes back on — that dark blue dress I made out
of a piece of linen you gave me, a piece left over from the last suit
you had us make. I don't know if you ever saw my dress, it was the
new style with a deep V in the back, a pinched waist, and it came
just a few inches below my knee. I had a patent leather clutch
bag and some high heel shoes that matched my dress that I had
found at a thrift store over in Coatesville. With some lipstick on
and my hair combed and rolled into a bun on the side, I looked

good that morning. It wasn't that I wanted to be attractive, I just wanted to look strong for what I was going to do. I fastened the butterscotch-colored bracelet on my wrist that Willie had given me back when he gave me the sewing machine and stepped out into the living room. Everybody looked at me puzzled, but nobody asked questions and I just told them I'd be back after a while. My heart was racing and my back and sides were burning with pain, but I knew I had to do this. I couldn't wait any longer to play my last card.

The walk from Bertha's house to town was hard enough for me to get hot and sweaty. My dress wilted and wet circles formed under my arms. As I walked, I was planning out what to say. I didn't know if he would be in his office, but I had to take my chances. The longer I walked, the more my ribcage hurt and the harder it was for me to get my breath, but I would not turn back. I walked on toward the square in downtown Edgefield and got to where I could see the white cottage which was his law office. Keep on going, I kept telling myself. Mrs. Alexander, I thought about you saying not to wait for somebody to open doors for you but to knock the doors down yourself. I was about to knock a door down.

A man and woman were walking toward me on the sidewalk. I didn't step off. I had got so used to doing that in Philadelphia. The man told me, "Girl, you better watch where you goin'." I heard him spit on the pavement soon as he got past me, but it didn't hurt me. I got to Strom's office and stood still a second, then got ahold of the rail until I could get my breath, walked up the steps, and knocked on the door. Chair legs scraped across the floor and the door opened. There he stood. He didn't speak, so I said, "Hello, Mr. Strom."

"Carrie? What are you doing here? Come in here." He looked outside as he took my arm and pulled me in, shut the door, and told me "Have a seat." He hadn't changed. A good suit, starched shirt, silk tie and had his hair combed back neat and oiled. He was clean-shaven like I always saw him. There were the books, the desk, the college diploma, same as before. The smell of that shave lotion came across the desk when the fan behind him blew a wave of warm air across my face. I was almost sick. I swallowed it down. He pushed some books and papers apart to clear a space on the desk between us.

"How you getting along, sweetheart? How you like living in the North? You are still living up North, aren't you?"

I just got to the point. "I came to talk to you about Essie Mae."

"How *is* your daughter?" he asked me.

I told him, "My daughter is sixteen years old and has been living in Coatesville, Pennsylvania, all these years with my sister Mary. She's doing very well. She's smart. She's won awards in school and been elected president of some of her clubs."

"That's wonderful. You must be proud of her. So, what brings you here today? You haven't come back to stay in Edgefield?"

"No. I'm just here for a few days. We had a death in the family. I lost my sister Mae. But Essie Mae. There's something needs to be settled about her before I leave this time."

"What do you have in mind?"

"Essie Mae wants to go to college. I don't have money to send her. The only way for her to get to do what I never could is for you to pay for it."

It took all my nerve to say what I said next. I told him, "I won't stay quiet any longer about who she is unless you say you will educate her. She deserves that from the man who is her father. Who has never acknowledged her. Who would rather keep her out of sight out of mind so he can pursue his own goals. But I have a goal, too, and it is for her. I will get help from somewhere even if I have to let people know who she is. Do you want me to do that, or will you get her educated and see she never goes hungry — ever? She may not want your help. She might not want anything to do with you or anything from you. But I want to know that if she wants it and needs it, she will get it." I was dizzy by then and my heart was about to explode. Strom looked down at his gold fountain pen like he wasn't sure what it was for.

Then he asked me, "Why do you think anyone would believe you?"

I told him, "We can see who they believe if you want to."

"I thought we had an agreement about this situation already."

He sat there, breathing heavy through his nose. He looked at the wall behind me. Someone knocked on the door. Strom got up fast and opened it. He told the man standing there, "I'll see you shortly. Go have a cup of coffee at the drugstore and come back in half an hour. And tell them to put it on my tab." I saw the man peer around Strom to get a look at me, then Strom stepped sideways to block his view and shut the door. He sat back down across from me and looked at me.

"I don't like what you're doing. I don't like it at all. There ain't a man in South Carolina who hadn't messed with a nigra girl at one time or other. How do you know it was me? Might not a been me. This type thing can't be proven."

My face went hot when he said that, but I had to stay calm. "She looks like you. Anyone could look at her and tell." Then I told him about you, Mrs. Alexander. "I have a friend who is a Philadelphia lawyer who will help me prove you are her father. Her name is Mrs. Sadie Alexander. You heard of her?" He moved back a little. He knows who you are. I told him, "My child was lost to me when she was six months old. That's a loss I will never get over. I hope you never know what it's like to lose a child. But you can do this for Essie Mae — see she gets to go to college." I told him, "She's your daughter. You can do that so easy, Mr. Strom, but it will be life-changing for her."

I had done it. What could he do? He would not risk his career. He looked at me, lips tight, shook his head, then got up and walked to the window and looked out.

"I'm bringing her here tomorrow to meet you."

I rose and went to the door, opened it myself and walked out with neither of us saying anything else. I don't think he would ever realize that, although what he did to me was an insignificant part of his life, it was the defining moment in mine.

Outside, the hot morning sun hit my face. When I reached for the handrail, my bracelet got caught on a nail and broke where the brass links joined. It fell into the grass down by the railing. The man who had come to the door earlier was standing, waiting at the foot of the stairs, so I didn't stoop to search for it.

I looked straight ahead and walked back to Bertha's. Coming toward me on the sidewalk were a man and woman, but I stayed on my side of the sidewalk and walked past them. I felt like I was an invisible spirit moving through time a few inches above the sidewalk. When I got to Bertha's porch, I could hear all of them talking inside, but when I walked into the house, silence. No one spoke, but the looks on their faces said they all wondered what was going on. I told everybody, "I need to rest a while," and went into Bertha's room where it was dark and cool and took my clothes and shoes and stockings off and got in her bed under a cool sheet. The last thing I saw before I went to sleep was a crescent moon in the daytime sky out the window by the bed. I fell into a black, dreamless sleep I had waited for for over sixteen years.

The next morning at Bertha's I felt pretty good. My back didn't hurt, and my head wasn't aching. Getting that visit behind me had given me such a sense of relief. I ate a cold biscuit Bertha had made that morning and went in the living room to get Essie Mae up and tell her we had a visit to make. She was asleep on a pallet Bertha had fixed for her. It had got hot in the night and Essie Mae's skin was glistening, her hair dark, heavy, thick and smooth. I stood looking at her while she slept. She would go to college. Maybe become a teacher. I believed Strom would keep his word, either out of a sense of duty or out of fear. It wouldn't matter which. I knew he didn't want the world to know about Essie Mae. If the world had known about her, he might have lost his chance to be governor.

I reached down and put my hand on Essie Mae's back and told her, "Put your funeral clothes back on. I'm taking you to meet someone."

She rose up off her pallet slow, looking sideways at me, her brow wrinkled, suspicious. "Who?"

I told her, "You'll see. Just put your dress back on and comb your hair." But she wanted to wear a new dress Bertha had given her — a pale yellow shirtwaist dress fitted in the bodice with a gathered skirt and a narrow belt at the waist. When she put it on, I saw her for the first time as a young woman. I put a little lipstick on her to bring some color to her face. From the trip down and the funeral and all the visiting we'd done, we were all tired, looking a little peaked. I had dressed already. I wore my dark blue funeral dress though. I put on lipstick, too. I still wanted to look as strong as I could. By 9:30 a. m. we were walking to town. Edgefield was humid and the sun pressed us down as we walked to town that morning. Sweat was trickling down my sides. The smell of the hog pens was very faint, but still there.

"Who we going to meet?" She had to walk fast to keep up with me.

Now I would tell her: "I'm taking you to meet your father."

"Carrie, wait! What are you talking about? I don't want to do that right now!" She grabbed my arm in both her hands and tried to stop me, her nails raking my arm as I kept walking.

I stopped, took her elbow in my hands, told her "Come on, we can do this."

Strom opened the door before we had got to the top step of his law office. We walked in. I tried to keep things moving. "Essie Mae, this is Mr. Strom Thurmond, your father." Total silence from all three of us.

Then she said, "Hello, sir" so quiet I barely heard her.

Strom said, "Hello, young lady. Why, you're even prettier than your mother. Carrie, you have a lovely daughter," always able to ease into his role of flattering people. He said, "Won't y'all have a seat" and waved his hand toward two chairs across the desk from his chair. He started asking her questions, "How do you like school? What subjects are you taking? Do you study Latin?" Her answers were quiet and polite, brief. He told her, "Don't neglect your diet. A diet of vegetables is best. Not much bread. You must take exercise every day." I watched him look at her, but I couldn't tell what he was thinking. Was he proud of her? Was he in awe of her? He shook her hand when we got up to go. He wished us well, said, "Good luck, darlin'." He patted her on the head, took hold of her elbow, and moved us toward the door. Essie Mae went out first. Before I went out the door, I looked him in the eye to see if I could read his answer. He nodded.

Essie Mae talked more on the walk back to Bertha's than usual. She started asking the questions about him that I had expected she would come around to asking like "Was he in love with you? Was he with you when you had me? Do you think he will want to see me again? Does he have more children?" I told her, "We'll talk about all this. I promise."

———◆———

You rest now, Carrie. I'll be back tomorrow.

Chapter Twenty-four

THAT NIGHT AFTER ESSIE MAE MET HER FATHER, I THOUGHT back to when I left Willie Clark and took Willie Junior with me. I knew that before we left, I owed it to both of them to take Willie Junior to see his father, too.

We had one more day in Edgefield before our trip back to Coatesville. When Essie Mae and I got back to Bertha's, I took Willie out on the porch and told him we were going to go see his daddy. He jumped up and down, making me realize that he had missed his daddy more than I knew. Bertha's boyfriend Jake said he would take us out there.

The next morning, we set out to go to the Clarks' farm. Willie Junior climbed in the wagon first and I got in beside him. Jake kindly tried to make conversation with us and asked Willie how he liked living up North. Willie told him. "OK I guess," but he didn't open up much as we bumped along the road a few miles out into the country to the Clarks' land. I tell you I had some emotions on that ride out. Willie Junior was almost nine by then and his daddy hadn't seen him in two years. He had sent Willie Junior letters telling him about new cousins he had that had been born after we left, about his grandparents, about the livestock and crops the family raised. At the end of each letter, he told Willie he could come back home whenever he wanted to. All in all, he had been a good father. He sent a few dollars each time with a "PS give this money to your mama."

When we got to the top of the road leading down to the house, I didn't see anybody. As our wagon began to stir up dust though, I could see someone open the screen door. It was Willie's mama, Genie. She stood still there on the porch with her hand shielding her eyes from the sun. I felt tears welling up in my eyes just looking at her. I said, "Willie, there's your grandmama."

What do you say to someone you haven't seen in two years and whose son you left and whose grandson you took with you? I wondered how she would feel about seeing me. Once Jake drew the mule up to stop, everything happened so fast and so natural though. When Genie saw who I was, she took a step toward us, stopped for a second, then started walking fast toward the wagon wiping her hands down the sides of her apron. Willie Junior jumped down and ran to her, almost knocked her over, while I climbed down and walked into her open arms. Genie hugged me so hard both of us stumbled a little. It felt almost like home. She wiped tears off her face with the heel of her hand, smiling and crying at the same time as her focus went to Willie Junior. "Oh Lord is this that boy I have missed so very much!" Then Genie hugged Willie Junior for a long time, her eyes closed as she stroked the back of his head. She kept saying, "Thank you Lord, thank you Lord."

Then I saw behind Genie -- Willie Clark. I looked down at the ground. I was caught up in emotion. Willie came to Willie Junior, and pulled him into himself, tears on his face. "My son is here, Mama. Our boy is here. Can't believe it. Oh God, I can't believe it. Boy, you have grown too much!" Willie Junior jumped up into his daddy's arms and wrapped his arms and legs around him. Then I was aware of someone else standing quiet on the porch. A woman who looked about my same age came down the steps and walked over to Willie. He put an arm around her and said, "Lustra, this is my son, Willie Junior, and his mother, Carrie."

She held out her hand. "Hi Willie! Boy, have I heard a lot about you!" Then to me, "Nice to meet you."

I was undone. Words that came out of my mouth were "Lustra. What a beautiful name." I had wondered if Willie had found someone else. She stood between Willie and Genie. Genie looked down at the ground but then took Willie Junior's hand and told us, "Y'all come on inside" and Willie ran to get his father from down in the pasture. Genie talked to Willie Junior, asking him about school, friends, got him telling her what all he had been up to. Thank goodness because I didn't know what to say to Lustra. She looked into my eyes and told me quietly, "I'm sorry to hear about your sister passing," then reached out and pressed my hand.

Soon Willie's father Jerry came in, overjoyed to see Willie Junior, and as kind to me as Genie had been. We stayed for dinner and talk got a little easier. When Willie pushed his chair back and stood and came over to me, my heart beat fast. As he walked toward the door, the others stood, and Lustra went to helping Genie with dishes. Jerry lifted Willie Junior and told him. "I got a surprise to show you! Baby calf born this week. You can help me pick out a name for her." I followed Willie to the porch. He stood facing me and took both my hands.

"When you comin' back, Carrie?"

"I got no plans to come back, Willie."

"You got to come back. We still married, or have you forgot?"

"I know that, Willie, but I can't come back now. I'm glad you've got someone else."

"Lustra's a good person. She knows things between her and me might be just temporary though. She knows about us."

"You should stay with her Willie. I'll bet she cares deeply about you if she's been willing to stay with you knowing we're still married. But Willie, I'm not coming back."

"Then you got to leave Willie Junior here."

"I can't do that right now, Willie. You got to let me keep him with me. There's gonna come a time when he will need to come back here, though. You stay in touch with him. Keep sending him letters so he stays aware of you and this place. I got to know he can come back here if anything happens to me. Willie, I'm not well. Don't anybody know about it. I swear I will see he gets back here with y'all. Please trust me. I've got to keep him 'til I can't do it anymore."

"Carrie, what's wrong? You come back here. We'll see you get well. What you talking about? Carrie, tell me what you talking about!"

I couldn't tell him everything and Bertha's boyfriend who had brought us here showed up while we were talking. Leaving was hard. We all hugged each other. Willie hugged me and quietly told me "Take care of yourself. Write me when you get back up there and tell me what's going on."

"OK, I will."

Lustra hugged me, too. As I climbed into Jake's wagon, Willie Junior said, "Daddy, you can come stay with us in Pennsylvania." I got a lump in my throat. The best thing to do was for us to get in the wagon and head back to Bertha's and not look back.

In the wagon on the way back to Bertha's, I found myself considering that Lustra might one day be Willie Junior's stepmother. Instead of jealousy, I felt relief. Mrs. Alexander, I think when you're sick, you get a sixth sense about people, about a lot of things. I could tell she was a good person.

We left Bertha's early the next morning to catch the bus back to Columbia where we would get on the train. I got Willie Junior and Essie Mae up early. Mary was already awake. We had said our goodbyes the night before and didn't wake Bertha. It would have been hard to say goodbye again.

Most of that long trip back everybody was solemn and tired. Essie Mae and Willie played some games out the window like counting cows and I spy. They slept off and on, and once we got past Washington, I felt like we had the longest stretch behind us. Mary slept most of the way. I kept my arm resting on the side of the car at the window and rested my head there. I closed my eyes but couldn't sleep. My back hurt too much.

Over the next few months, Essie Mae would want me to tell her about how it happened that Strom was her father. When did I meet him? Did his family know about her? She wanted to believe he had cared for me. I did tell her, "He might've stayed in touch with me if his daddy hadn't sent him away after you were born." She was proud of him in a way, I could tell. Well, let her be proud of him. After all, half of who she is comes from him. And he is a smart and famous person, respected and admired by many people. It's going to be complicated for her, though. She'll have a long time to digest everything. All I care about is that she'll get the chance to live for herself.

I thought about those migrating butterflies Velma taught us about — about how not all of them complete the journey. I got farther on the journey than my own mother did. I won't get to the destination either, but I hope Essie Mae will.

Chapter Twenty-five

Roy was glad when we got back. He told me he had worried I might decide to stay in Edgefield. I said, "There was no chance of that happening." Me and Roy were together a while longer, then the US joined the war. Before we ate supper one night, he told me he wanted to talk to me about something. I got Willie Junior to bed and came back in the living room and we sat down on the couch. He took my hands and told me, "Carrie, I been happiest I ever been with you here. I never knew anybody like you. I want us to have a long life together. But there's something I've decided I'm gonna do to make life best as it can be. A man from the army been coming to the post office trying to get people to sign up. And today I volunteered to join the army."

I remember going, "You what? Why? No. Please. You can't go! You too old anyway, aren't you? They want young boys! You don't need to do that, Roy."

But Roy told me, "I come back from fighting in a war for this country and everything gonna be different. Nobody gonna see a man as second-class if he volunteered and put his life on the line for the country. Besides, if Americans don't beat the Germans, no telling what will become of the world. I got to do this, Carrie. It's gonna be a different world when I get back, and you and me will have a good life."

"But what if you don't come back?" I asked. Then Roy joked and teased me and tried to lighten up the conversation. He had made up his mind.

I got one letter from Roy not long after he left. It's one thing I keep with me. I still get it out and read it from time to time. Let me show you.

> *My Dearest Carrie,*
>
> *I hope you are doing ok. I am fine. We arrived in Fort Meade, Maryland, last Tuesday. We spend the day doing drills and getting instruction on everything from shining our boots and making up our cots to reading maps. From here we will go south to Tennessee to Camp Tyson. We been told that we have to keep the curtains drawn at the windows on the train when we go south because whites have shot at trains carrying negro soldiers. Word is that at Camp Tyson we will train for six weeks to do a secret mission. If I can tell you about it, I will next time I write. A man in my squad heard we'll be doing something has to do with balloons that are bigger than busses, but that doesn't seem logical. Most colored men in the army will be driving trucks,*

loading ships, or cleaning latrines, but we're told we are lucky to get this assignment, whatever it is.

I hope Willie Junior and Essie Mae and Mary are all OK. Tell Willie be good and me and him are going to see the Philadelphia Stars play soon as I get back, watch our man Jud Wilson hit a homerun.

Don't worry about me, just take care of yourself. I left a little money hid in a cabinet there over top of the stove. Use it whenever you need to. I know you work hard at your job but try to rest when you get home and get rid of that pain you got in your back.

I sure do miss you and all the things we did. In my cot at night, I close my eyes and reach my hand out and imagine I am touching your beautiful face and I pull you close to me. I think we ought to get married when I get back. Please think about it. Figure out how we can make that happen, OK?

All my love, Roy.

I would love to see Roy one more time, but I don't hold out for that any longer. No telling what happened to him or where his body lies. If it was blown to bits or if he burned or got shot down in a plane into the ocean. Or did he find someone over there he fell in love with and decide to stay. I think about him at night. I get his letter out and read it. But after that letter, I have never heard from him again. I wasn't his next of kin, so I never got word and don't know if he was killed overseas or if he just stayed there or what. His people in Kentucky might have heard something, but they didn't know me, wouldn't have known to tell me.

Bertha wrote me regular for a few months after we made that trip down to Edgefield. She told me Strom had resigned from the bench to serve in the army. He is now famous as a hero from landing on the beach at Normandy.

I have read that a battalion of colored men who started out at Tyson like Roy did were among the first to land at Normandy, handling huge balloons along the coast of Normandy, protecting the soldiers who were landing on the beaches there. I wonder if that's what Roy was talking about in his letter. I wonder if Roy died there.

That's been nearly six years ago now and colored men who fought in the war have come back but not much has changed for them. Some things have even got worse. Mrs. Taggart's husband heard that whites in the South didn't like to see colored men wearing their army uniforms after they came back home. Said wearing that uniform made colored men feel equal to whites and white men wanted to nip those feelings in the bud. You hear that French people didn't treat colored soldiers any different from how they treated white soldiers. Stories have even got out that colored soldiers had love affairs with white French women during the war and, now they're back, they're lusty for white women at home. Some colored soldiers have been lynched and many more have been beaten and shot.

Our Aunt Bertha wrote my sister Mary about a colored soldier from Batesburg — that's about twenty miles from where we lived in Edgefield. His name was Isaac Woodard. This man had an honorable discharge from the US Army. He was on his way home on a Greyhound bus, wearing his uniform, and when he asked to use the restroom at one of the stops, he was arrested. A white sheriff beat him and gouged his eyes out with a blackjack, then left him in a jail cell all that night. They took him to the city court the next morning where he was fined for drunkenness and disorderly conduct.

Roy hoped he would be respected when he got back, but he never got back. If Roy had come back, he would've been very disappointed. Strom, on the other hand, came back a war hero. He received a Bronze Star and a Purple Heart and ran for governor of South Carolina. And he won, too, as you know. Last year he got married to a girl Essie Mae's same age named Jean. There was an article about him in *Life* magazine, his picture in there with him wearing white short pants and standing on his head to show how strong and fit he is. His wife, Jean, is standing there beside him smiling. She is pretty and young.

Strom has got real popular in the South with folks who want to keep segregation. Mary told me some say he's going to run for President. Since President Truman has come out for Civil Rights, a lot of the Democrats have broken away from the Democrat party, started the Dixiecrat party, Strom being one of them. He says Civil Rights should be left up to the states.

———◆———

Carrie, every conversation we have strengthens my desire to help your daughter get her education. Thank you for giving me an opportunity to help. I'll see you tomorrow.

Chapter Twenty-six

Thank you for coming, Mrs. Alexander. Today I was thinking back about a night Mary and Essie Mae came to see me and Willie Junior at Roy's place in Chester, not long before Essie Mae left for college and when I still had hope for Roy to come back. Anyway, that day after work I went to the butcher shop and bought four thick pork chops and then stopped and got some cabbage and potatoes at the farmers market down the street. I went to the grocery near here and bought real butter, flour, eggs, and sugar, a can of pineapple, and a coconut. I would make Essie Mae's favorite — a three-layer pineapple coconut cake. I got home and made biscuits the way Aunt Lucy taught me, as big as your hand. I buttered the tops before I put them in the stove so they would come out brown and crispy. I found Roy's hammer to bust open the coconut and saved the milk to pour over the cake to make it moist. That night I had my family with me, treating them to a good supper with money I made working at a job I loved.

Willie Junior told me, "Mama, I love that pork chop. It's the best thing I ever had to eat." It made me think about my Aunt Lucy and how, unlike me just getting the butcher to wrap them up, she slaughtered those hogs herself in a smokehouse out behind her house. She would butcher three or four hogs late in the fall once it got cold enough, so we had meat about every day. Aunt Lucy was strong. You know a hog weighs about three hundred pounds and when you go to butcher one, you have to stun it first. Aunt Lucy would hit it between the eyes with a mallet, then one of her nephews would help her slit its throat. Once you do that, the hog starts to thrashing around. Then they'd raise it up with a winch by a big oak tree in the backyard to let it bleed. I'd be wanting to go inside by this time because I couldn't ever get used to the smell, or to the sight of that hog suffering so, steam rising up from its blood. Once they emptied its belly, my job started. They'd give me the intestines, tell me, "Stick a stick down in there, turn it inside out, and wash it out real good in that tub of water." Those would be fried chitterlings later on, and they stunk! But by time Aunt Lucy had made sausage out of that hog, I had put the awful part out of my mind, and I would eat it and love it. Some things are like that — you might can put the bad part out your mind if there's a good part comes after.

The rest of that evening we were all at peace. Essie Mae and Willie played gin rummy with a deck of cards Roy had. I was as satisfied as I could be.

While we smoked our cigarettes, Mary told me Strom had contacted her when he was up here for the Democratic convention in Philadelphia and asked her to bring Essie Mae to see him at the hotel where he was staying. I don't know why he didn't contact me to bring her. Maybe he didn't know how to get in touch with me. Mary said they took a cab there then rode the elevator up to a meeting room. Strom greeted them, "Come in and have a seat." Essie Mae had just graduated from high school in Chester — that was three years ago now back in 1945 — and he asked her about her college plans then told her he thought she should come to South Carolina State in Orangeburg, South Carolina. He told them people were encouraging him to run for governor. Out there on the porch, we got chilly and went inside with Mary still telling me about what all Strom had said to Essie Mae. "Are you eating vegetables and drinking lots of water? No coffee or tea. Are you exercising?" She said he told her, "I weigh the same now as I did when I was about your age. I take exercise every day. Never miss a day. And no caffeine. No alcohol or tobacco. You got to keep yourself clean, body and mind." She said as they were leaving, he handed her a sealed envelope. When she opened it after they left, she found a hundred dollars inside. Right then, Willie Junior, who had been listening to every word Mary was telling us, scrambled up and started doing jumping jacks and singing "I'm so healthy! I drink water! I take exercise!" Essie Mae spurted out a mouthful of soda and we all got to laughing so hard we fell into a pile on the floor and laughed 'til we cried. Once we settled down quiet again, I asked them, "Did he ask about me while y'all were there?" We had all stopped laughing by then. Essie Mae looked away and told me, "I don't believe so."

Mrs. Alexander, do you think Strom asked Mary to bring Essie Mae to see him then because he cared about her? Maybe he did, maybe he just wanted to test her out, see what was her attitude toward him, assure himself she wasn't a threat? Maybe he wanted to start persuading her to go to college in Orangeburg so he could keep track of her and keep her satisfied. And maybe he cared about her. Maybe he still does. Whatever reason, she's there now, going to college, and that's all that matters to me. She's going to have a chance.

I've never told Essie Mae I got him to promise he'd do that for her, or why he made that promise. I rather she think he's doing it because he cares about her. Maybe he does care about her. How could he not? I might be wrong not to tell her the whole truth. Either way, I know you'll see he keeps his word.

I will, Carrie. I told you when we first met that I never looked for anybody to hold the door open for me. You remembered that. So, if we have to knock this door down, we will.

Chapter Twenty-seven

ME AND WILLIE STAYED IN ROY'S PLACE UNTIL I HAD TO COME here to the hospital. I've used up all the money I came up here with and I've missed a lot of work, but Mrs. Taggart has kept paying me anyway. Mary's taking care of Willie Junior, but she will see he gets home to Edgefield with his daddy.

I don't remember exactly when I got to feeling so sick because I tried to ignore it or just thought I was tired from working and bending over my worktable to cut fabric and sitting for hours at a time sewing. I been having pains in my back for years, but once I started to get worse, I got to itching all over. Nearly drove me crazy and I would put lotion all over myself but that didn't help. Then I started having pain that never let up all in my back and sides, between my ribs, in my hips. Then I got headaches and couldn't sleep good at night. I was passing blood when I finally got to the doctor.

I kept working and some days I felt good and thought I was getting better. Some days, though, I could hardly make it through a day with so much pain. Mrs. Taggart cut back on the work she gave me, mostly gave me piece work, not anything where I'd have to lean over the cutting table.

A few weeks ago, I came in to work and Mrs. Taggart said, "Carrie, I made you an appointment to see my own doctor." First thing I thought of was I can't pay for that. She told me, "Don't worry about the cost. I'll take care of it." A couple days later a cab pulled up to the shop and Mrs. Taggart walked me out to it, told the driver where to take me, and paid him.

I was scared. A nurse took me to a room and told me to get undressed and get up on a table. She put a sheet over me and stood there until the doctor came in. He examined me and asked me so many questions. He sat down in a chair beside me and told me he thought I had renal failure and that I needed to have some tests. I knew right then that was what my mother died from. I had been handed a death sentence. Coming out of there my mind was spinning. How long could I keep working? Would I tell anybody? Mrs. Taggart would ask me what the doctor said. Mary has known for a long time that I've been getting sicker. We watched our mother together get worse and worse, and we know what could happen to me. But I wouldn't tell anybody else. Not for as long as I could keep from it. The tests would have to wait. Maybe the doctor was wrong.

A few weeks later, I passed out at work. Mrs. Taggart may have told you. Three or four women were in the shop talking, trying on clothes we'd altered, crowded around the mirror on the back of the door in the room I work in. One of them lit a cigarette, which you probably know Mrs. Taggart doesn't like because it makes all the clothes and fabrics smell. Mrs. Taggart asked her to please put the cigarette out, but I had already breathed enough of it to make me feel sick. I got so hot. My head began to spin around, and the noise of those ladies talking sounded far away. Next thing I know, Mrs. Taggart's got me sitting up on the floor, leaning me against the wall, fanning me, giving me cold water. That's when she called a taxi to bring me here to the hospital. It had started raining. Holding an umbrella over us and holding onto me, she hailed a cab and helped me climb in, told the driver to take me to the Philadelphia General Hospital. Told me she would close the shop and come herself as soon as she could.

Mary told me they used to call this hospital Old Blockley from when it was the poor house. The doctors and nurses here treat people kind and they try to help everybody — even folks like me who can't pay a dime. They call us Mr. and Mrs. So-and-so. If I was in Edgefield, there wouldn't be a hospital that would even admit a colored person. Thank God I left that place. I thank God for the Philadelphia General Hospital and for the doctor who examined me and admitted me, and for the nurse who helped me out of my clothes and into the hospital gown. She gave me a clean sheet and helped me pull it up over my legs. The doctor rubbed his hands around the stethoscope to warm it up before he put in on my back. He lifted my feet up on to the bed and pressed easy on my stomach, trying not to hurt me, but still I cried out when he did that. He asked me did anyone in my family ever have kidney disease and I told him about my own mother who had died when I was fifteen. I told him about Mrs. Taggart's doctor telling me I had renal failure. He held my arm out and tapped on the inside of my elbow 'til he saw where a vein was, and he slipped a needle in that was connected to a tube that ran up to a glass bottle of clear liquid hanging from a pole. He held both my hands in his and told me he'd give me something that might help with the swelling. My wedding band, thin as wire, had begun to cut into my finger. He told me he would have no choice but to cut it if I couldn't get it off by the next morning.

They brought me into this ward where the cots are lined up against the wall. Just like he said, Dr. Drexler came by my bed the next morning after the nurse had sponged me off and he wrote down in my chart for them to give me something for pain. He had brought a little pair of pliers and took my hand to see if the swelling had gone down enough to get my ring off, but it hadn't. He pushed one side of the pliers up under the ring and snipped the metal, then bent the ring apart enough to take it off my finger and told the nurse to put it with my belongings. He put a salve on the raw flesh where the ring had dug into my skin. He told me there was not much treatment for the kind of kidney disease I have but that they would try to keep me comfortable. I asked him if I'm going to die and he just looked away, I guess he didn't know what to say. Nothing *to* say. Every morning when I wake up and feel my heart still beating, I feel some relief. Then again, I hope I die in my sleep.

The nurse who brings me a pill in the night isn't gentle like the doctor is. She helps me onto the metal bedpan, but she pulls it out from under me so fast when I'm through that sometimes it spills out a little into my bed. I know she has to hurry. I hope it doesn't smell bad. Something in here smells bad.

I had some tests today, an x-ray of my kidneys. The doctor gave me more medicine for pain. When the pain gets ahead of the medicine and I need more please, they tell me I have to wait until morning. Then I can't sleep, and the night is so long. It's hot in here. There's a sweet, sour smell. I feel like I've smelled it before. You hear patients cough and moan in the night. A nurse walks through the ward twice during the night, sometimes whispering to ask what you need, checking on everybody. I'll bet she walks ten miles every night. Her shoes don't make a sound. That clock on the far wall by the night light takes hours for the hand to move twenty minutes. I'm swollen all the time. I dream about my mother more than about anything else. I dreamed we walk out of the hospital together and I take her downtown here in Philadelphia, and we go to the fountain at a drug store where I buy her a vanilla ice cream soda with chocolate syrup and nuts in a sweet sauce and whip cream and a cherry on top. She doesn't want to eat it because then it will be gone. She's smiling. Her hair is plaited in neat rows against her head. Her skin is moist and shining. We ease off the stools and walk to a dress shop where she tries on a flowery dress and a yellow hat, one of those cloche hats you roll the brim back. She never speaks. There's no one in the store but us. As we're walking back to our house, which has become our old house on Brooks Street, she fades 'til she disappears. I call her but I can't get her back. Everywhere I look now seems like the world is divided into people who are living and people who are dying. And I am with those who are dying. I think about Mama and I know she had to have suffered before we knew how sick she was.

Chapter Twenty-eight

CARRIE, I WAS A LITTLE LATE GETTING OUT OF COURT TODAY. MY CLIENT, a businessman, got into a relationship with his secretary and now she's pregnant and her baby will be delivered just a few weeks shy of the baby he is having with his wife. Folks can surely get their lives in a mess.

———◆———

Yes, something can happen in one day that changes a person's life from then on. Both of my children have been here to see me. I wish they had come at a time when you were here so you could have met them. Willie Junior had gone back to South Carolina and stayed with his daddy last summer, but he's back with Mary now, and she's gonna stay behind him 'til he finishes high school. He came to see me soon as he found out I was in here. I told him Mary has the thin gold ring, cut in two, in my things and for him to keep it since it was his daddy gave it to me.

Essie Mae came up a few days ago. Mary wrote and told her they had admitted me in the hospital, and she got on a train and came right up. She brought flowers but the nurse made her leave them outside the ward. She's in college now down at South Carolina State in Orangeburg and so far, Strom has paid her way. She has a boyfriend who is in law school. She told me she's doing good and hopes to graduate next year. Strom has visited her at college a few times. She said a black limousine pulls up at the college and everybody wonders who it is. The president of the college calls Essie Mae to his office and that's where she sees her father in private. Strom has told the college president that Essie Mae is an old family friend. She said he gives her money in an envelope and talks to her for a while. He tells her what all he is doing as governor. She tells me he extended the school year to nine months in South Carolina for white as well as colored children. He told her he helped get welfare for children who need it if they were still in school. She wants to see the good in him and have me see it, too. After all, he is her father.

He once asked her how it feels to be the daughter of the governor. She says it causes a lot of talk at the college when he comes and people start guessing that one of the women students is his daughter, but they haven't guessed it's her. They think it's another girl in her sorority. Sometimes it seems like maybe he wants people to hear the rumors that he has a colored daughter. Like you heard them. Like those men in Edgefield who kidded him when they saw me leaving his office that time. I heard he bragged to somebody once that he had deep roots in the colored community. Still, he's coming to see her. And he's still paying her way.

Before you got here today the lady in the cot next to me died. Earlier yesterday she kept begging for a drink of water. I can't get up from here or I would've got her water, and I called out, too, as loud as I could, and two nurses came and helped her drink, one holding the cup to her mouth and one raising her head. They stayed with her while she died. I had to turn away at the end. She tried to breathe but nothing but a rattling sound came out until it was over. A little later two workers came and covered her with a sheet and took her out. She was right next to me there – just a few feet away.

Last night my grandmother came to me in a dream again. I was on trial in the courthouse in Edgefield. The windows were all raised and the sharp smell of the hog pens was burning my eyes. A lawyer was asking me where I was on such-and-such a day and how I learned to read and write and how I learned to sew, why I let my baby girl go way back then, why I left Edgefield and my husband, why I took my son away from his father. I just kept shaking my head, trying to say "I had to. I had to," but no words would come up out of my throat. Then my grandmother came for me and got me by the elbow and walked me through the courtroom and out into the square. Just a ways down from that monument to the Confederate dead, I see another monument -- a man up on a pedestal looking out over the square, holding what looks like a book in his left hand. My grandmother takes me over to a tree like the one I dreamed about long ago. We lie down on the earth beneath it and look up into green leaves that are trembling to be alive. The air is so pure it lifts us off the ground when we breathe it in. My grandmother tells me, "I found out who planted this tree. It was you, Carrie."

I want to thank you for hearing me, Mrs. Alexander, and for getting all this written down. I wanted somebody to know I did the best I could. My teacher, Velma, once told us, "I want y'all to remember these four things: use your mind, do unto others as you would have them do unto you, don't waste your money, and buy some land and hold on to it, even if it's just a little patch." I've used my mind and I never wasted my money. I've tried to do unto others as I would want them to do unto me, but I had to do some things to get by that I wouldn't want done to me. I never got any land, but I did get that promise for my daughter that I hope will be worth more than land. So far, he has kept his promise, but you'll make sure he does? I am so proud of Essie Mae. I'm thankful for her. I am glad she was born. I hope I made things up to her. Mrs. Alexander, I've got to go now. My mother's here. You'll keep all this in case Essie Mae needs your help?

I will, Carrie.

Epilogue

CARRIE BUTLER DIED OF RENAL FAILURE IN THE POVERTY WARD of the Philadelphia General Hospital in October 1948. She was thirty-eight years old. Her funeral was held at her sister Mary's church. She was buried in Chester, Pennsylvania.

That same year, Strom Thurmond ran for President of the United States as the States Rights Democratic Party candidate, a Dixiecrat, and made the famous speech in which he declared, "All the laws of Washington and all the bayonets of the army cannot force the Negro into our homes, our schools, our churches, and our places of recreation and amusement." He served as Governor of South Carolina from 1947-1951. He was United States Senator from 1954 until his death in 2003.

By reliable accounts, Thurmond paid Essie Mae Washington-Williams' tuition to South Carolina State College. After he became governor, he visited her there occasionally. He wrote a letter of recommendation for her husband, Julius Williams, to get into law school. According to Essie Mae Washington-Williams' memoir, he continued to provide some financial support for her and some of her children throughout his life. In 1970, he was the first member of Congress in SC to hire a Black staff member. He helped gain federal funding for poor people in rural, predominantly Black areas, an act which attracted the support of some Black activists. Between 1972 and 1996, he attracted more and more Black supporters. He also supported making Martin Luther King, Jr.'s, birthday a federal holiday.

In 1999, a monument to Thurmond was built on the State House grounds in Columbia, South Carolina, a nine-foot bronze figure of him standing on an eight-foot base. Soon after his death in Edgefield, SC, in 2003 at the age of 100, Essie Mae Washington-Williams, herself almost seventy-eight, publicly confirmed her relationship to Thurmond. The Thurmond family acknowledged her as their relative forthwith. The Thurmond monument was amended in 2005 to add the name of Essie Mae Washington-Williams and to change the number of his children from four to five.

No known photograph of Carrie Butler exists.

ACKNOWLEDGEMENTS

So many people have helped me accomplish writing *Leaving Edgefield*. Foremost, is my dear friend Marilyn Clarkson who researched extensively, accompanied me to Edgefield many times, and read and re-read the manuscript and offered invaluable suggestions. I couldn't have written this book without her.

Another friend, author Susan Zurenda, provided the impetus for me to begin the book by repeating to me, "Just start writing!" As simple as it sounds, that advice made me take the first step of putting words on paper. An experienced writer herself, Susan was also an early reader who gave me valuable advice about writing and publishing.

Many thanks to my niece, Katherine Weaver, who introduced me to her writer/brother, Ben Rogers. Ben painstakingly pored through an early draft and offered hundreds of professional comments that helped me begin to mold the material into a structured, meaningful story.

Thanks to former colleague, astute teacher, author, and poet, Frances Hardy, who agreed to read an early draft for authenticity. I was so grateful and relieved when she told me, "It didn't make me cringe."

Other readers whose input has been invaluable include Catherine Ayers; The Honorable Tommy Hughston and Mrs. Mary Ann Hughston; Julie Garrett; Margaret Garrett; author Peter

Schmitt; author Charles Dallara; author Josephine Humphreys; my daughter, Charlotte Pilato; my daughter-in-law, Jamie Hooker; my brother, Billy Weaver; and my husband, Dempsey Hooker.

Support came in many different ways from Phil and Mark Clarkson, Ben Nixon, John Nixon, Chip and Alice Smith, Katie Walker, Bronwyn Cox, Ann Rogers, Gabe Pilato, and Emily Knowles.

Heartfelt thanks to authors Michel Stone, Jeffrey Blount, and Michele Moore whose own works inspired me and who were generous enough to offer words of support for *Leaving Edgefield*.

Thanks to author John Warley who gave me an introduction to former Evening Post Books executive editor Michael Nolan, and to Michael, the first person at EPB to recommend my book for publication. Thanks to Elizabeth Hollerith at Evening Post for help in early stages, and infinite thanks to Jacob Hollifield, my brilliant editor at Evening Post Books.

ABOUT CAROLYN W. HOOKER

Carolyn W. Hooker, a native of Spartanburg, South Carolina, received a B.S. Degree in Education and an M.A. Degree in English from the University of South Carolina. A former English teacher with over thirty years' experience on the high school and college level, she lives in Charleston, South Carolina, with her husband. This is her first novel.

ABOUT WRITING *LEAVING EDGEFIELD*

Having grown up, raised children, and lived in Upstate South Carolina for most of my life, I have long been drawn to the region's distinctive political and cultural history. I came of age during a national turning point, when this corner of the South — and those who held power here — were slowly brought into the light.

In 2003, Essie Mae Washington-Williams extended that light with her memoir *Dear Senator* (ReganBooks, 2005), deepening my interest in the social politics of 20th-century South Carolina. Years of research and reflective drives to and from the Edgefield County archives and beyond gave shape to Carrie's world in my notes and on the page. I traced her story through books, census records, and articles, attempting to envision her with respect and authenticity.

My hope is that this imagining of Carrie Butler's life projects even a fraction of the illumination these documents brought to my own understanding of this place—and that, though no image of her survives, her quiet resistance will not be forgotten.

WORKS CONSULTED

"African American Burial Society Cemeteries." Preservation Society of Charleston. Preservationsociety.org, Accessed 11 Sept. 2024.

Allen, Louise. "Bettis Academy." *South Carolina Encyclopedia.* USC, Institute for Southern Studies. 17 May 2016. http://www.scencyclopedia.org/sce/entries/bettis-academy/, Accessed 21 May 2023.

Ardrey, Carl, President of Southern Railway Historical Association. E-mail interview. Received by Carolyn Hooker, 4 Dec. 2024.

"Autosomal Dominant Polycystic Kidney Disease." *National Institute of Diabetes and Digestive and Kidney Diseases.* 2017. *14 June 2017. https://pkdcure.org,* Accessed 14 June 2017.

Banks, Nina. "Sadie Alexander: Race, Historical Memory, and Black Liberation." *YouTube.* Uploaded by Bucknell University Dartmouth, 14 Oct. 2021, youtube.com/watch?v=CEA52-k59ms. Accessed 23 Apr. 2025.

Bass, Jack and Marilyn W. Thompson. *Ol' Strom: An Unauthorized Biography of Strom Thurmond. Longstreet, 1998.*

---. *Strom: The Complicated Personal and Political Life of Strom Thurmond.* Public Affairs. 2005.

Bay, Mia. *Traveling Black: A Story of Race and Resistance.* Belknap, 2021.

Bengston, Bill. "Innovation and Locomotion: Smithsonian Exhibit Focuses on Train History." *Post and Courier"* 12 Nov. 2024. Postandcourier.com.

"The Blinding of Isaac Woodard." *American Experience.* PBS, 30 Mar. 2021.

Bruck, David L. "The Four Men Strom Thurmond Sent to the Chair." *Washington Post,* 26 Apr. 1981. https://washingtonpost.com, Accessed 18 Mar. 2017.

"Carrie Butler 1910-1948" (plus additional 82 names of relatives of Carrie Butler). Ancestry.com. 2017-2022. https://www.ancestry.com. Accessed 2022.

Childress, Alice. *Like One of the Family: Conversations from a Domestic's Life*. Beacon, 1986.

Cobb, Jelani. "The Segregationist's Daughter." *The New Yorker*. 7 Feb. 2013. http://newyorker.com, Accessed 21 Apr. 2018.

Cohodas, Nadine. *Strom Thurmond & the Politics of Southern Change*. Simon & Schuster, 1993.

Crenshaw, Kimberlé Williams. "Was Strom a Rapist?" *The Nation*. 26 Feb. 2004. http:thenation.com, Accessed 21 Apr. 2018.

Crespino, Joseph. *Strom Thurmond's America*. Hill and Wang, 2012.

Edgar, Walter. *South Carolina: A History*. U of SC Press, 1998.

Edgefield County Archives. Personal visit. Mar. 2017.

Family of Francis Butler Simkins, *Francis Butler Simkins 1897-1966: Historian of the South*. Columbia, SC: State Printing, N.d.

Ferleger, Louis. "Sharecropping Contracts in the Late Nineteenth-Century South." *Agricultural History*, vol. 67, no. 3, 1993, pp. 31-46. JSTOR, jstor.org. Accessed 29 Apr. 2025.

Gates, Henry Louis, Jr. "Exactly How 'Black' Is Black America?" *The Root*. N.p. 11 Feb. 2013. www.theroot.com, Accessed 9 Aug. 2022.

Georgia Historical Society. "Marker Monday: Ware High School: Civil Rights Milestone." Georgiahistory.com. Accessed 23 June 2023.

Gettleman, Jeffrey. "The Nation: Strom Thurmond's Child; Old Times There Are Not Forgotten." *The New York Times*. 21 Dec. 2003. https://www.nytimes.ccom/2003/12/21/weekinreview/, Accessed 28 Apr. 2017.

Glass, Andrew. "Supreme Court Bars Racial Bias by Railroads, April 28, 1941." *Politico*. 28 Apr. 2019, politico.com, Accessed 9 Oct. 2024.

Gordon-Reed, Annette. *Thomas Jefferson & Sally Hemings: An American Controversy*. U. of Virginia, 1997. Kindle.

---. "Thurmond Story Tells Harsh Truths." *Women's eNews.* N.p. 24 Dec. 2003. www.womensenews.org, Accessed 14 Mar. 2017.

Gregory, James. *The Southern Diaspora: How the Great Migrations of Black and White Southerners Transformed America.* U of North Carolina, 2006. Kindle.

Harris, Middleton A., ed. *The Black Book (35ᵗʰ Anniversary Edition).* Random House, 2009.

Hervieux, Linda. *Forgotten: The Untold Story of D-Day's Black Heroes, at Home and at War.* Harper, 2016.

Hillinger, Charles. "The Sweet Chariot Swings Low – A Study of Black Burial Rites." *Los Angeles Times.* 5 July 1989, latimes.com, Accessed 4 Dec. 2024.

Hunter, Marcus Anthony. "Black Philly After the Philadelphia Negro." *Sage Journals.* 18 Feb. 2014. https://contexts.org/issues/winter-2014/, Accessed 19 Feb. 2018.

Hutchinson, Sikivu. *Godless Americana: Race and Religious Rebels.* Los Angeles: Infidel Books, 2013. Kindle.

Jones, Jacqueline. *Labor of Love, Labor of Sorrow.* Basic Books, 1985.

Katkins, Mara. "Almshouses (Poorhouses)." *The Encyclopedia of Greater Philadelphia.* 2002. http://philadelphiaencyclopedia.org, Accessed 21 Apr. 2018.

Lerner, Gerda, ed. *Black Women in White America: A Documentary History.* Vintage, 1992.

"Logues and Timmermans: S. C.'s Bloodiest Family Feud Still Vivid." *Goupstate.com.* 2 Oct. 1988. http://www.goupstate.com/story/news/1988/10/2/88, Accessed 21 May 2023.

The Lucy Craft Laney Museum of Black History. "The Golden Blocks." http://lucycraftlaneymuseum.com. Accessed 23 June 2023.

McCarthy, Jack. "Remembering the Downbeat: 1940s Progressive Philly Jazz Club." 7 Apr. 2014. Hidden City. hiddencityphila.org. Accessed 18 July 2025.

"Monarch Butterfly." *National Wildlife Federation.* http://www.nwf.org, Accessed 30 June 2017.

Newby, I. A. *Black Carolinians: A History of Blacks in South Carolina from 1895 to 1968.* U of SC Press, 19??

Obasogie, Osagie. *Anything But a Hypocrite: Interactional Musings on Race, Colorblindness, and the Redemption of Strom Thurmond,* 14 *Yale J. L. & Feminism* 451. 2006. https://repository.uchastings.edu/faculty_scholarship/1355, Accessed 21 Apr. 2018.

Outterson, Kevin. "Tragedy and Remedy: Reparations for Disparities in Black Health." *DePaul Journal of Health Care Law,* vol. 9, no. 1, 2005. https://via.library.depaul.edu/jhcl/vol9/iss1/4, Accessed 17 May 2018.

Palmer, Alex. "This Segregated Railway Car Offers a Visceral Reminder of the Jim Crow Era. *Smithsonian Magazine.* 13 June 2016. *Smithsonianmag.com,* Accessed 14 June 2023.

Rainsford, Bettis, Sr. "Coming to Terms with Our History." *The Edgefield Advertiser.* 3 Aug. 2015, edgefieldadvertiser.com, Accessed 4 Dec. 2024.

---. "Critics Who Question Strom Thurmond's Legacy Should Take a Deeper Look at His Legacy." *The State,* 02 July 2020. Amp.thestate.com, Accessed 20 Nov. 2024.

Roberson, Frank, Ph. D. *What Is the Conclusion of the Whole Matter? A Perspective on the Politics of Senator J. Strom Thurmond.* North Augusta, SC, FGR, 2004.

"Sadie Tanner Mossell Alexander." AZQuotes.com. Wind and Fly LTD, 2023. http: azquores.com/author/33526-Sadie_Tanner_Mossell_Alexander, Accessed 21 May 2023.

Short, R. J. Duke. *The Centennial Senator: True Stories of Strom Thurmond from the People Who Knew Him Best.* Office of Juvenile Justice and Delinquency Prevention (OJJDP). U. S. Department of Justice. 2006.

Simkins, Francis Butler. *Memoirs of Litchwood "I Have Things to Tell": Francis Butler Simkins Remembers the Edgefield of His Youth.* Edgefield County Historical Society. 2016.

South Carolina Department of Agriculture, Commerce, and Industries. *Handbook of South Carolina*. SC State Library. 1907. N.p. dc.statelibrary.sc.gov, Accessed 11 Nov. 2017.

Staples, Brent. "Medical Racism." *The New York Times*. 13 Oct. 2014. Accessed 17 May 2017.

Thompson, Marilyn W. "Thurmond: The Girl from Edgefield." *The Washington Post. 4 Aug. 1992*. 22 June 2017. https://www.washingtonpost.com/archives, Accessed 22 June 2017.

---. "What a Family Secret Begat: Essie, Strom, and Me." *The Washington Post*. 21 Dec. 2003. https://www.washingtonpost.com/archives, Accessed 22 June 2017.

Thurmond, Strom. Interview. By James G. Banks. *Southern Oral History Program Collection (#4007): How Strom Thurmond Learned Hard Work and Politics in South Carolina*. 20 July 1978. *Docsouth.unc.edu, Accessed* 12 June 2023.

Todd, Leonard. *Carolina Clay: The Life and Legend of the Slave Potter Dave*. W.W. Norton, 2008.

"Trailblazers, Yesterday & Today: Alice Fisher and Jean C. Whelan, PhD., R.N." *The Woodlands* Official Blog, 24 Apr. 2014.woodlandsphila.org. Accessed 14 June 2023.

"Ware High School: Civil Rights Milestone." *The Historical Marker Database*. 16 June 2016. 23 https://hmdb.org, Accessed 23 May 2017.

Washington-Williams, Essie Mae and William Stadiem. *Dear Senator: A Memoir by the Daughter of Strom Thurmond*. Regan Books, 2005.

Wilkerson, Isabel. *Caste: The Origins of Our Discontents*. Random House, 2020.

---. *The Warmth of Other Suns: The Epic Story of America's Great Migration. Random House, 2010*.